AND
WHEN
I DIE

Russel D McLean

CONTRABAND

Contraband is an imprint of Saraband

Published by Saraband,
Suite 202, 98 Woodlands Road
Glasgow, G3 6HB

www.saraband.net

ISBN: 9781910192573
ebook: 9781910192580

Printed in the EU on sustainably sourced paper.

10 9 8 7 6 5 4 3 2 1

This one's for

Jay Stringer
and
Dave White

*In honour of their infamous procrastination-inducing emails
(without which, I'd have finished this months earlier).
(I don't know where they get the time to finish
their own books, either.)*

The Other Side of Town

Glasgow
2011

A suburban street in the Southside. Tenements all around. Middle-income workers, migrant communities. Shops shifting groceries at markdowns and takeaways selling kebabs and chips with gravy.

The man walks out of his one-bedroom flat. He's big, and walks leading with his shoulders, head held high. Posture perfect. Dressed in dark jeans and a red shirt that he wears un-tucked. On his feet, heavy boots that are scuffed from use. Hard to tell what he does for a living, if anything.

Looking the way he does, you figure he has money, but he's not a lawyer or a doctor, not living round here. He's not in sales. Doesn't have the smarm or the cheap polyester suit. He's not a shop worker or a labourer. Doesn't have the right look or the right walk.

What he is, is dangerous.

You know that by looking at him. The walk tells you that this is a man you do not mess with.

He's big. Not fat. Just big. The kind of chest that makes you think of Superman, deflecting bullets. Hands big enough that they could dig a grave. No real expression on his face; not happy, not sad, not angry. Maybe he's waiting to see how he feels today.

On the street, he looks up at the sky, as though expecting rain. But the sun is out. Most people would smile when they realise this. A sunny day in Glasgow – anywhere in Scotland, really – is something to be celebrated. But he merely looks up and then back down again with no change in his mood. He walks to a black Skoda: one of the newer models, not the old rust-buckets. He looks around again, but it's merely habit. The big man has clearly learned to be cautious over the years. A doctor or lawyer or sales-man or manual labourer would not be cautious.

But despite all the precautions, he doesn't see the people in the grey Megane further down the street. They've been watching him since he came out of the building. Both of them coked up. One is trying hard not to vomit, while the other barely notices the drugs in his system. Truth is, the second man needs a regular hit just to keep himself stable. The first is only high under duress.

What he's doing is barely keeping himself together.

This is the last time, he thinks. *After today, it's over.*

They wait. They watch.

The big man gets into the car. Closes the door. Turns the key in the ignition.

There's a moment when he seems to realise that something's wrong. He twists in his seat, reaches for the door.

When the explosion comes, it's bigger than either of the two coked up men expect. It pushes at the cars to the front and rear, and blows out the windows of the nearest building. Twisted scraps of metal arc into the air, trailing flames and sparks.

The two men in the car don't bother to see if the big man's dead.

They just drive off. One of them vomiting violently into his own lap.

One

Pay to the Piper

Two days after the car bomb

John

I take a look in the rear view. Remind myself who I am.

'Your name is John Grogan. You are a police detective. You no longer have to pretend.'

Like slipping off a mask you've been wearing for too long, you're no longer sure what the real you looks like. So, which one of us is me? The undercover cop? The would-be-crooked financial advisor?

The murderer?

Three distinct people, really. That's the problem. At first, it was like playing a part. Now, some days, it comes so natural it's hard to remember who I really am.

If I ever knew.

Maybe I was always a murderer. Or... No. He was a mistake. He was...he wasn't me. He was the coke. He was something outside my control. That's what he was.

The face in the mirror looks back, eyes wide with panic. Pale, red rings under the eyes from lack of sleep. There was an incident two days ago No matter who I think I am, I can't figure a way to deal with the fallout. All I can do is ride this one out. Hope that I come through in one piece.

The face in the mirror hardens. The man looking back at me has been in hiding for over two years now. He's disgusted with some of what he knows, some of what he's seen. And more, he's disgusted that he can't talk about it. That there were things that had to be done in order to maintain my...*our*...cover. Am I losing my grip on sanity? Who could blame me if I was?

Over two years now I've lived with the idea that one day everything I've worked for will come crashing down. Maybe I'll say something out of turn. Maybe I'll forget who I'm supposed to be. Maybe some lag I arrested donkey's years ago when I was doing the uniform beat will put two and two together, realise where he's seen my face.

6

Here's what I know after two years deep undercover:

Derek Scobie is a psychopath. The kind of psychopath Hannibal Lecter has nightmares about. The good doctor ate people's liver, but at least he was cultured and witty. Derek doesn't even have that going for him. Only person worse than him is his youngest son, Anthony.

Anthony Scobie makes his old man look like a kids' TV presenter – a cuddly, benign uncle.

And let's not even talk about Raymond. Not yet.

Because Raymond's still alive.

Raymond's still alive.

The words are a chant, a mantra, a reassurance.

Raymond's still alive.

Alive is a matter of degrees, and after what happened to him two days ago, alive could be a very loose term indeed.

Whatever, I have to see him. Understand the condition he's in. Try and figure out how I'm going to explain all of this. I'm so far off the reservation, not even Google Maps can find me now.

This is uncharted territory. Nothing in the manuals about what to do when you fake a man's death and then fail to inform the detective in charge.

Not like I don't have my reasons. All I need to do is get Ray to speak. Spill his guts. Metaphorically, of course. Although the state he's in after the explosion, we could be talking literally as well.

If he talks, then I figure I can call in my superiors, admit to my mistakes. Take a slap on the wrist and hope to hell that they don't believe a word Derek and Anthony tell them.

Aye. Right.

I take a look in the rear view again, see those stranger's eyes staring back at me. Cold, unforgiving.

He knows the truth. There's no way out of what I've done. That whatever happens next, I'm the one who has to deal with the consequences. And I can't blame it on my cover. Because here's the thing – when you're undercover, you're still the one in the driving

7

seat. Your cover isn't independent. He's an extension of you.

Maybe that was my problem all along. Me and my cover, we found the places where we merged, became the same person.

The question is begged: which one was the cover? The cop or the crook?

I open the car door, climb out. The cold air hits hard. Ice shards in my lungs. I look at the A&E building just a few hundred yards away.

Think about running.

Figure I've been doing that most of my life. Maybe now's when I finally face up to what I've done.

Kat

The BBC are talking about Raymond. Of course they are.

'Raymond Scobie's death is believed to be connected to gang violence in the city of Glasgow. His murder is just the latest in a series of escalating...'

I switch channels. *Undercover Boss USA*. Fine.

I don't have to think about Raymond. Just watch some rich, out-of-touch guy with 1980s hair throw his workers a few meaningless platitudes after pretending he's worked as one of them for an hour of telly.

By the end, I'm crying. Can feel the tears on my face. Didn't even realise it was happening. They're not tears of empathy, either.

I swing my legs over the edge of the king-size bed and stand up. Traffic noises outside the window. I go over, look out at the city.

Glasgow.

Six months I've been gone, figuring that's it, I'm done. And now I'm back. Once a Scobie, always a Scobie.

I shower. The water is on full, smacking my skin, pummelling out all the tears and the sadness. The heat cocoons me, and, for a while, it's like I've escaped the world.

Something about hotel showers: they always feel cocooned from reality.

When I come out, there's a curdling in my stomach. Heavier than butterflies. A reminder of reality.

I fire up the laptop. It's old and clunky, takes its time booting. When I finally log onto Gmail, I catch a number of messages from work telling me to take my time before coming back. One from Lesley saying, *Call me if you need to talk.* I smile. A little guilty. It's been a few weeks since we talked. Somehow, I always feel that makes me a bad friend.

Lesley and I came through nursing college together. She stayed on the wards, while I went into admin. She was better able to cope with the horrors of ward work. Maybe that was surprising to some people. They figured I should have been used to blood. It's in the Scobie family, after all.

John

First time I met Raymond, he looked at me the same way you might look at a dog who just took a dump on your rug. Ray wore a cheap suit, no tie, shirt just the right side of ironed. He chewed his lower lip every so often. I took him for an ex-smoker looking for a new bad habit.

I'd later realise he hated wearing suits. His brother and his father insisted, however, so he pulled the same one out time and again for social occasions.

It didn't fit him. Few clothes did. His frame was too large in all the wrong places. He wasn't designed to fit in to the world. He wasn't built to be normal. He would never fade into the background.

He was big. Features hacked out of the side of a mountain. He couldn't crack a smile. Or any expression, really. Just looking at him made something tickle at the base of my neck, made me want to turn and run. There were all kinds of rumours about Ray. It was my job to sort out what little of the truth there was about him. He was the gangster's bogeyman. The kind of person who kept grown men lying awake at night with their bedside lamps on.

The oldest son of Derek Scobie, Ray had a rep for death. Known colloquially as the Ghost. Hard to imagine, given his size, that he could kill people and simply disappear like so much mist, but however he got the reputation, you believed it the moment you met him. The very sight of him touched something primal.

The SCDEA have a large file of unsolved gangland murders they like Ray for, but they've never been able to place him at the scene or find a single piece of corroborating evidence. Never been a hair left behind, a fingerprint smudged, a flake of skin beneath a fingernail.

If he has a signature, it's that he prefers to kill from a distance. The weapons and the calibres of the bullets vary from case to case. He might have a stash, but no-one knows where it is. Raids on Ray's one bedroom in Govanhill always turned up less than nothing, leading to red faces all round and mumbled, insincere apologies from the local constabulary.

But he's a killer. No doubt. You look at him and you know. One third of what Crawford had refers as the Scobie's own Holy Trinity:

The Father.

The Son.

The Holy Terror.

I forced my hand out, offered it to him like a dentist reaching into a lion's mouth to pull out a rotten molar. His shake was lighter than expected. As though he didn't really want to touch me. But social convention had him cornered.

He was a tough man to work out. Didn't really talk, barely made eye contact with anyone. Carried a glass, but barely took a sip from it. Didn't like social convention. Didn't really like people. Probably what made it so easy for him to kill.

The first words I said to him were, 'How're you?' A quick and easy greeting, not giving too much away. He didn't say anything.

We were in a bar, which was maybe why he felt he had to keep holding onto that glass. Our introduction wasn't going well. I was there as Kat's plus one, had been doing the introductory rounds, feeling like finally this operation was getting ready to pay off. But unlike everyone else in the room, it seemed Ray wasn't willing to take me at face value. And with Kat off to the bathroom, I was on my own trying to make small talk with the most dangerous man in Glasgow, maybe even Scotland as a whole.

Ray looked at me and said, 'Think you could do it? A stretch like White's?' The question surprised me. Not just because it wasn't the kind of question you ask your cousin's boyfriend first time you meet him. But because he was assuming I understood his world.

Dave White had been 'away'. Someone told me, as the newcomer, that he'd been 'touring the world'. They laughed when they said it. I acted innocent, the way I was supposed to, still not feeling the truth behind my cover, still waiting for the moment when they spotted the copper behind my eyes. But I knew what they meant. White had been away a long time. But all he'd seen of the world was what he might have read in books or seen on a communal telly.

I said, 'I'd try not to get caught in the first place.'

Ray just nodded, not saying anything. He'd asked his question. Got his answer.

I tried not to shrink inside my skin.

• • •

The thing in ward 45's isolation room doesn't look like the man I met two years earlier. Barely looks like a man at all.

His skin has been burned, near enough melted. What hair is left appears in wispy patches across his skull. He's hooked up to pipes and feeds, like a medical experiment gone badly wrong. Or Frankenstein's monster. Brought back to life only to suffer.

I did this to him. Coked up, whatever, I don't have any excuses. I lit the blue touch paper and walked away. Figured he was dead.

Criminals always return to the scene of the crime. In the end,

I'm no different.

Soon as I could dump Anthony, I did. Doubled back to see what was happening. Dropped character, became the cop I used to be. Slipping into a way of walking and talking I'd figured I might have forgotten.

Helped that I knew the officer in charge on the scene. Asked him to me a favour. Told him it was in the name of a sting operation. He fudged the paperwork, told me I owed him. That it was his balls on the line.

'It'll be sorted out in the end,' I said.

He trusted me, too.

Never trust an undercover. We'll lie to anyone. It's in our nature.

Thing is, I was still high. Anthony Scobie's condition for me helping plant the device. His way of making sure I could be trusted.

Hitting coke, I always felt like I was standing two or three steps behind my body, watching it as though it was controlled by someone else.

When this all hits the fan, I think I could lose a friend or two.

More than that.

The heart monitor beeps steady. There are footsteps outside the door. Hushed voices echo from elsewhere in the ward.

But we're alone.

Just me and Ray.

The ghost. The man who should be dead.

His chart reads *John Doe*, of course. No-one knows who he really is. I see people walk past the room sometimes, looking in, curious as to why this man is locked away from view.

I wonder how much he remembers. Did he see us that morning? Did he know that we were watching him?

I lean over him.

He forces one eye open. A chaotic mess of broken capillaries. His lips part. The skin cracks. 'Here to finish the job?' His voice is low, each word a struggle.

I shake my head.

His words don't mean he knows anything. Just that he remembers who I am. Of course, if he remembers too much, then I'm as fucked as he is.

I reach inside my jacket and pull out something even I haven't seen in a long time. My identity and badge number. They've been in a storage locker for almost two years now. When I looked at them this morning, I had to convince myself they didn't belong to someone else.

He breaks into a coughing fit.

I sit patiently and let it pass.

Underneath my shirt, I'm drowning in sweat. My arms and legs are shaking. My heart could be playing the best of Miles Davis, the way it syncopates. My ribcage aches.

I take a deep breath. 'They think you betrayed them, Ray. I saw the evidence. Big, regular deposits in your personal account. Came through a number of subsidiaries, but I traced it. Came from that pasty fuck, Buchan.'

'They're family.' He coughs again. Then, a deep breath. Both eyes open now. Staring right at me. Not once breaking contact. 'And….sod…Buchan. Never…paid me nothing. Wouldn't work for…him. Family. Fucking family.'

'Think family really means anything to your lot?'

But it does. It means everything. The Scobies are tight. Derek always talks about family loyalty. Bit of a monomaniac that way. Only way the Scobies could be any closer is by inbreeding. Makes me glad the old goat never had any daughters.

Both Ray's eyes close. His breathing shallows out. Those monitors register slower beats. His whole body relaxes, like he's drifting into sleep. I reach for the panic button, thinking that everything I've done over the past two years has been for nothing.

If he dies, then everything I've done becomes little more than the punchline to a bad joke.

'Tell me,' Ray says, opening his eyes, twisting his lips into what might be a smile. Suddenly alive. 'They know? About you?'

The bomb should have killed him. Should have done its job. But it didn't. And right at this moment, I wish it had.

'Does...' and I think he smiles, 'Kat...know?'

I stand up. Still unable to believe he's alive, never mind able to talk.

The heart monitor hits overdrive. The cough shakes and rattles Ray's body. The bed joins in, threatens to break apart under the strain of his gigantic frame entering some kind of seizure.

The expression on his face does not change.

I run out into the hall, flag down a nurse. She takes one look at Ray, thrashing around on that bed, calls for help. Tells me to wait somewhere else.

I slip into a waiting room. Spend some time pacing before finally grabbing a chair. Kill time reading leaflets that tell me how cancer will kill a frightening number of people I know, and that the odds are I've got some form of it too. I re-learn how to recognise a stroke. Read advice for family members, for recently diagnosed patients. Begin to think about what hidden dangers lurk in my body. My stomach seizes. For a moment, I imagine it might be a tumour.

After half an hour, the doctor on-call comes in to talk to me. A serious-looking man with thick glasses. Not much more than nineteen or twenty. At his age I probably looked every bit as serious, believed myself king of the world.

In a way, I still do.

'Your Mister Doe,' he says, no pre-amble, 'is a minor miracle.'

Not the way I would describe the cold-blooded bastard. Not the way anyone who's ever met him – especially in a professional sense – would ever describe him. But the young doctor does, with a sense of awe and what I think might be admiration.

'He should be dead,' the doctor says. 'At the very least in a coma. Massive internal injuries, and those burns... If that was me, I'd be screaming for morphine every two seconds. But he just...he just takes it.'

'He can actually handle that amount of pain?' I understand his reaction. There's stoical, then there's impressive.

The doctor sits down in one of the chairs just along from me and adjusts his glasses. I lean forward. Old cop instincts coming back. Treating this like an interview. I'm the man in the mirror now. Slipping back into his skin, using him to get what I need. I need to lose the stance and the attitude when I leave. I've spent two years building a cover, and I'm not going to blow it. Until I know the precise prognosis and how useful Ray's going to be to my case, I can't afford the luxury of relaxation.

Of course, even when this is all over, I don't know that I'll ever be able to relax again.

Kat

Twelve years old. Face in the mud. Grit on my lips, between my teeth. A weight on my back. Fingers in my hair, pulling, twisting.

And the yells:

Scabies Scobie! Scabies Scobie!

What you get for a family name like ours. And having red hair at twelve. Long red hair that your mother tells you is beautiful, but really just makes you a target for bullies like Jenny Hanson.

Scabies Scobie! Scabies Scobie!

Jenny was the one doing all the pushing, the one sitting on the small of my back, pressing down with all her not inconsiderable weight.

She smelled of rank BO, but no-one told her that. She could beat the boys when it came to a fight, and her gang worshipped her as much they were afraid she would turn on them next. She was that kind of bully, that kind of monster.

'All bullies,' Mum told me, would tell me, 'are afraid.'

Never made me feel better, though. When I thought of bullies I thought of Jenny Hanson. Maybe she was afraid, but it didn't stop her from beating the tar out of any girl (or boy) she took a dislike to.

I had the stupid name. The stupid hair. And teachers liked me. She was on me like a heat-seeking missile. Making me eat mud. Laughing at my name. Pressing down on the small of my back with her knee. Telling me I was going to be a spinal case. Or dead. And no-one would care. Because I was a 'filthy fucking ginge!'

Someone shouted, 'Ginger Minger!' with the enthusiasm of the scared.

Other voices joined in.

I started choking. Couldn't breathe. The grit was in the back of my throat. When I swallowed, it scraped against the soft tissue, made me want to scream.

Was I going to die?

That's what I believed. Truly, honestly.

And then the chanting stopped. Silence struck the playground. The pressure on my back eased momentarily. I forced my head to twist round so I could see what was happening.

Some of the assembled girls were making a break for it. Startled gazelles who just realised there's a predator bearing down on them.

A voice rumbled, 'What d'you think you're doing?'

Jenny Hanson clambered off me. Hurt worse than when she jumped onto my back in the first place. I rolled over, tried to clamber back onto my feet with some degree of dignity. Failed miserably.

Jenny Hanson quaked – wobbled, really – with fear. The man had big shoulders, big hands and a stillness about him that spoke of absolute, terrifying control.

I smiled, even though the taste of grit and the backwash of blood frightened me when I swallowed.

My protector. My saviour. My cousin.

Ray.

Even at the age of twelve, I knew there was something not quite right about my family, the way that some people behaved around them. But I couldn't quite put my finger on the enormity of what it

16

all meant. It would take me until I was fourteen or fifteen to really figure it out.

Ray had a reputation, I knew that. He was big and strong and sometimes, when you looked at him you thought about monsters and giants from the fairy stories you read as a child.

He was dangerous. And Jenny knew it, too.

She looked at him, eyes wide with fear, maybe even a kind of attraction. I was just beginning to notice boys, and if Ray wasn't my cousin, I might have had a little crush on him, even though I'd never dare to act on it. Because he gave out all the wrong signals. He was dangerous. More dangerous than any boy I'd ever met before or since.

Ray said, 'She's my cousin. Family. Leave her alone'

Jenny didn't say anything. She turned and ran. Maybe she even cried. I certainly hoped so.

Ray came over to me. 'Go home. Wash up. Tell me if that wee cow ever raises her voice to you again.'

I told him I would. Ray walked away.

'We look out for own,' Uncle Derek used to say. For years I saw this as a good thing. Persuaded myself that all the other stuff, all the things I heard were exaggerated or that they had been done for the sake of the family.

The Scobies like to believe in their own myths.

Even when they're a lie.

• • •

I've been thinking about Ray a lot since I got the phone call. Uncle Derek on the other end of the line, telling me his son was dead. His words flat, still in shock.

The local papers have been filled with coverage of the investigation. The TV has broadcast endless footage of Uncle Derek, along with an old photo of Ray that makes him look like the son of Satan. Like he clawed his way up from the pits of Hell.

I know the truth about my family. They've done bad things. I

17

know that Uncle Derek's legitimate businesses shield him from other aspects of his life. I know that Ray wasn't as unemployed as he looked on paper.

I know all of the dirty laundry.

Sooner or later you need to make a decision: you either walk away or you get involved.

I walked away.

After John. After what they did to my life.

The decision should have been heartbreaking. Instead, it was simple. John did that. By choosing my family over me, by proving that all the Scobies do is corrupt, seduce and ruin everyone who gets involved with them.

That's not me. Never has been. Never will be.

Nothing like the betrayal of a lover to help you make those all-important decisions, to finally shove you down the road you always knew you should take and were too afraid to.

A new life out near Oban. Just the sea, my work, a quiet little apartment, a chance to finally become someone else.

And now I'm back.

I can't help it. It's in the blood. For everything that's happened, I can't not come back for Ray.

Death can bring any family back together.

Around me, people eat their breakfasts, talking in mostly hushed tones. Sometimes, the over-excited voice of a child peaks above the drone, but mostly people keep to themselves, conversation low around their own tables, as though afraid everyone else might be listening in.

I pull out my phone, check Facebook, find messages of support mixed with a few spiteful comments about how he had this coming. I unfriend the haters fast. Wonder about when people mistook rudeness for honesty.

My breakfast arrives. I put down the phone, face up on the table, and dig in. Bacon. Sausages. Beans. Potato scones. All in congealed fat, only lukewarm. I eat anyway.

My heart belongs to Glasgow. Where else could it belong, when a breakfast like this appeals more than the healthy continental spread across the other side of the room?

Someone is standing across the table from me. Waiting for me to notice their presence.

I look up from the bacon, swallow what I've been chewing.

He's maybe mid-thirties in a blue shirt, black waistcoat and dark jeans. Not quite heavyset, and I get the impression he's maybe been trying to lose some weight and succeeding.

'Can I help?'

'Kathryn Scobie?'

'Who are you?'

'Jay Stringer, *Glasgow Evening News*.'

'Go away.'

'I want to talk to you about your cousin.'

'I don't want to talk to you.'

'No-one does.'

'Are you surprised?'

'Please, I want to put a human face on this loss of life. Everyone's talking like Ray Scobie's a monster. I want to show that there were ordinary people out there who cared for him. You're not like the rest of your family, Ms Scobie. You work a normal job. Keep yourself to yourself. Work for the health service. You'll be able to put across a side of your cousin that our readers will –'

'If you know anything about me, Mister Stringer, you'll know that I no longer have anything to do with my family.'

'You left. And now you're back.'

There's a silence between us for a moment. I look at him. He looks back. On the plus side, he's not sitting down. He's not that presumptuous. I choose to believe that's because he has some decency in him.

'How did you find me?'

'It's what I do. I'm a reporter'

'That's not an answer. Besides, I thought modern reporters did

19

all their work behind a computer screen.'

Now he sits down. Probably thinks he's established rapport. Maybe to him this is flirting. I swallow one last mouthful of sausage. The plate's only half-finished, but I'm suddenly not hungry any more.

I stand up.

'Why'd you leave, Kathryn?'

Make for the lifts.

'Why'd you come back?'

Try to pretend I can't hear him.

John

'There's a condition,' the doctor tells me. 'It's rare. But it's real. An actual thing.' He's wide-eyed now. Finding someone with this condition, for him it's like me banging up one of the Krays.

'Congenital insensitivity to pain. Never seen it myself. But some people...their pain receptors don't work properly. They can take punishment like you wouldn't believe. Because they don't get all the signals to their brain telling them something's wrong. So you could...I mean...excuse me, this doesn't sound exactly textbook, but you need to know...you could kick them in the bollocks. Wearing steel-toes.' He sounds more than a little excited. Takes off his glasses and puts them back on again. He's a mass of tics. Makes me glad he's not a surgeon. 'And they wouldn't feel it. I mean, the subject just wouldn't care. They might notice, feel a dull ache, but it would be like me flicking you in the fleshy part of the arm. It just wouldn't matter.'

'You're telling me that this is Ra– uh, John Doe? He doesn't feel pain?'

'Your suspect? Yes.'

Suspect. No wonder he looks excited. Wee lad probably thinks he's in the midst of some glossy crime drama. *CSI Glasgow*, some bollocks like that.

'He's...a freak?'

The doctor hesitates. 'He's just...'

I nod. 'He's different.' Meaning the same thing.

The doctor nods. 'I've read case studies. First time I've met someone with his condition. Most of the time people with this family of symptoms don't live long. Pain is good for us, you know? Pain lets us know that something's wrong. So, for example, an itch in the eye, it's a kind of pain. But people like him, they're less likely to notice an itch. So the grit starts scratching the iris, but the subject doesn't feel anything...'

I got where he was going. 'He gets an infection?'

'And dies.'

'Sounds melodramatic.'

'Not really. That's why our instinct is to scratch, to get that bit of grit out. Like anything, if you leave it long enough, things get bad.' He smiles at me. 'Our first year lecturers at university liked to tell horror stories about patients who die from paper cuts and the like.'

I'm only half-listening now. Thinking about what Ray's condition means. He's always been distant, but I had assumed it was to do with his particular line of work. When you kill people for a living, you have every right to be paranoid.

But it was more than that; like Ray didn't quite understand other people. And if he didn't feel pain, maybe that made him more distanced than anyone could understand.

More of a monster, perhaps.

'Surely he'd need constant supervision?'

'When he was young, sure. They need to learn routine. Notice that things are wrong in other ways.'

'You don't have records for him?'

'Given the need for secrecy...you never gave us his name. No name, no medical records.'

21

Didn't matter. I knew almost everything there was to know about Raymond Alexander Scobie. There were gaps in his life that this big secret accounted for. When he was a child, he was kept hidden away by his father. Attended school in fits and bursts, never had much of an education. Why? It had always been an unanswered question. His brother, Anthony, had been brought up normally. So clearly something about Ray had been very different.

Was this the big secret? His condition?

I could understand why Derek would try to hide it. The Scobies were strong, and an illness like the one the Doctor described could be construed as a weakness by someone with the right kind of mind.

But all I could really think about was the idea of a man unable to feel pain. And wonder what else he couldn't feel.

•   •   •

I can see across to the Cathedral from here, out past the ancient structure and onto the Necropolis, what used to be known as Wester Craigs and then Fir Park. Now, the fir trees are gone and all you see are monuments to the departed. The view is marred by rain that streaks down the outside of the glass, same as fucking always.

I used to love this city. The rain was part of its charm. Now it's all part of the despair and the corruption.

Going undercover changed my perception, made me realise that what I saw was only part of the truth.

I switch Sims in my phone. Three days now I haven't checked this number. There are missed calls and messages. I don't need to listen to them. I know what they're about.

I can imagine the kind of chaos caused by my lack of response.

I have to wonder if they think I'm dead. By our last few meetings, they'd figured I was getting in too deep, that I was losing my grip. They'd asked me to pull the op and come home.

'Just a few more days,' I said, feeling I was getting close.

And then I was pulled in to that meeting with Scobie Sr. The

22

one where everything changed. Where I realised just how deep I really was.

But sometimes you have to face up to your mistakes.

I dial out.

Crawford answers immediately. 'Where have you been?'

'I'm sorry, I–'

'You know that in this situation extraction is –'

'I know the protocols. Burke drilled them into me. Thing is, I need to be allowed a degree of operational discretion. This particular scenario...' I trail off. I haven't thought this through.

'Yes?'

I take a deep breath. Look at the water marks on the outside of the glass. See the world distorted by rain. 'I think I can salvage this. This was a mess. But I think Ray's death...' I swallow, then. The lies are beginning to trip too easily from my lips. 'I have someone I can flip. I know it. Someone who can give us evidence.'

'Who?'

'Just trust me.'

'We need to extract you. The old man's just shown how far he's willing to go. Ordering the death of his son? And what's clear to me, you're not on the inside. He didn't tell you what he was planning.'

I press myself against the glass. It cools against my forehead. I close my eyes. I can feel the rain thudding outside. 'Maybe I had an idea,' I say, 'Maybe I just thought there was no way he could go through with it.'

'You don't have children.'

'No.'

'But you understand that, don't you? That no parent in their right mind would hurt their own child?'

'Yes.'

'That's the difference between Derek Scobie and any normal person. For all his talk about family, all his grand proclamations, the only person he will ever care about is Derek Scobie. You heard

23

him talking about anything close to what happened, you should have come to me.'

'Look–'

'Look, nothing! You need to come in.'

'Just give me time.'

'John…'

'Give me time.'

I hang up then. Take out the Sim. Put it back into the wallet. Swap back to the other number. Then head back down the corridor.

I can make this right. All of it.

There's still a chance.

• • •

I pull up a seat at Ray's bedside.

His eyes open. He turns his head, slowly. Still no expression. Those eyes move, but I can't tell what lies behind them. Give him a deck of cards, he could beat the house.

I say, 'The doctor thinks you can't feel pain.'

'I feel it.'

'He says you don't act like you do.'

'Not the same…as everyone else. Sensations. Dull.'

'It's a medical condition.'

'It's a…sick joke.'

'No wonder you escaped,' I say.

'I was…on fire.'

'I know.'

'They…. You…tried…to kill me.'

'Do you know why?'

'Does it matter?'

'Guess not.'

'You're…polis.' He spits the word out. Disgusted. More than reflex. Genuine hatred.

I don't say anything. He knows what I've done, who I am when the badge is hidden.

'He's my… father… Won't testify. Even though…'

'He's an old fucker who tried to kill you. Because of an imagined slight.' I pause. 'It was imagined, right? I don't think you went rogue. I believe you when you say you had nothing to do with Buchan. I think someone set you up. Someone in the family. Someone who had the means and the opportunity.'

'Even talk…like polis.' He makes a sound like the final death rattle of a wounded animal. Maybe it's a laugh. I've never heard him laugh before. 'Give…the man…an award.' He's wheezing. Laughing or dying. Either one would do him; long as it pissed me off. It takes him a moment to settle again. 'What happens…to me? If I keep quiet? About you.'

I hold my hands wide apart, show him that I have nothing to hide. 'I put in a good word about how co-operative you've been, anything could happen. The SCDEA want to talk to you. Fuck, everyone does. You co-operate, there every chance you could – '

'You're good,' Ray says. 'Fucking…car salesman. I'm not buying.'

'Just think about it, okay?' I say. 'You can't go back. This way you get to take revenge on these pricks.'

'Think…you liked it,' Ray says. 'The life. Think you forgot… who you were.'

I had been ready to get up leave, but his words root me to the chair. All I can do is look at him, and cock my head to indicate I don't understand what he's saying.

Except I do.

'You're not police,' Ray says. 'How you got in so deep. How much…do your bosses…know?'

I stand up, make to leave. Say, 'This is your chance to get revenge on whoever it was set you up. On the people who tried to kill you.'

'I'll have revenge,' he says. 'On my own…bloody…terms.'

• • •

Out in the corridor, I check my messages.

Three from Anthony:

25

Call me.

Fukin serious.

Call or you're a ded man.

I'm about to compose a reply when I hear someone running down the corridor. Their footsteps smack-smack-smack off the linoleum. Their breath echoes in sharp gasps.

I spin on my heels, see the young doctor, the one barely out of nappies. 'Detective!'

'Slow down.'

'Detective!' He's close enough that we could hug when he finally stops. His eyes are wide beneath the glasses. Sweating hard enough he could be a candidate for his own defibrillator.

'There's a problem with the patient.'

Christ!

I'm off and running before he can say anything else. Takes him a moment to work out what's going on and start running – maybe lolloping's a better word – to keep up with me. I say, 'What happened?'

'He's gone.' The words sputtering between wheezes

I slam on the brakes. 'What?'

'There's… I mean, one of my colleagues. The patient…the patient broke his neck.'

'I thought he was at death's door.'

When I'd left him, he was talking, he wasn't going anywhere. He might not have felt the pain, but that didn't mean he could just keep going like nothing was wrong.

'I don't… I've never…'

'He's killed a doctor?'

'And he's gone.'

It's too late to do anything. I know that in my heart.

It's been well past too late for days now. Since the bomb. Since I finally let the cover take control.

And now the situation's in freefall. All anyone can do is hang on and pray for a soft landing.

Two

Home Is Where the Hatred Is

Three days later

The day of the funeral

1223 – 1614

Kat

'We will now sing from the first hymn, selected by Ray's family for...'

I look up, remember where I am.

Jesus looks down at me.

Ray hated Church. Came only on sufferance, and even now he has to be carried in, brought down the aisle and placed before us. They asked me to carry a candle. I didn't think I could handle it, just wanted to be in the crowd, pay my respects in private.

I shouldn't be here.

Around me, people whisper in hushed tones, or sniff back tears.

Ray is dead.

Someone booby-trapped his car. Probably my uncle's business rivals. Buchan, maybe.

Tony, hyped up when he came to see me, said they saved money on cremation, at least. I reminded him that their father was a Catholic, that cremation wasn't the way forward.

He'd said, 'It'll make the coffin lighter.'

Not funny.

Of course no-one's saying a word about what really happened. Not to me, anyway. Because they all think that I don't know what's going on, that just because I stay out of the family business, I don't understand it.

I look around. There's something about Catholic churches really gets to me. The idolatry of it all, the sheer majesty of worship. Even in a poky 1960s-built church like this one, just off Merry Lee Road in Newlands, dwarfed by the local Church of Scotland which looks more like it should be the Catholic church to the casual observer.

When I was a girl, my mother took me to Paris to visit Notre Dame. The sheer size of the building had made me nauseous, utterly dwarfed by the idea that this really was God's House. That had been what I expected all churches to feel like, and something about our local Paris lost its majesty from the outside afterwards.

But inside our poky wee building, among the candles and reminders of the Son of God who died for our sins, I still get that feeling of panic and insignificance that hit me in the Parisian cathedral.

The church is packed. Not just immediate family. Also those who respect (more likely fear) my uncle. And a few reporters trying unsuccessfully to slot in, get a good snap of the big, bad gangster funeral.

I shouldn't be here.

• • •

'450 a month. Utilities, council tax, all that's your responsibility.'

I was only half-listening to what he was telling me. The flat had four walls and a roof and it would do for a while. Until I got settled.

'Do you have any questions?'

I shook my head. Went to the window. The view out onto the water was dramatic in the rain.

'The insulation is excellent.'

'Hmm.'

He came and stood beside me. 'It's very different from Glasgow up here. I mean, a lot quieter. A lot of the comforts of the city, well, they're not quite so readily available.'

Perfect. Exactly what I was looking for. After the last fight with John, I'd been wondering if it was a bad idea to act on my impulses. Handing in my notice at work, applying for a transfer, rushing up here like my life depended on it.

'Well?'

'Oh,' I said. 'I'll take it.'

Looking out at the water. Thinking about what it would be like to dive in. Let the water close in over my head. Feel that sensation of floating, freedom, escape from everything.

• • •

We were able to learn from an early age how to spot reporters and undercover police at any Scobie gathering. *Spot-the-hack* became a great way of breaking the boredom that came with funerals and birthday parties.

I see faces I recognise. Fat Dunc's a few rows back, looking uncomfortable in a shirt that's too small, threatening to choke the life out of him with the top button done up and that tie like a noose round his neck. There are food stains on his shirt. He's not been the same since Mary-Ann left. I think he's put on weight. Hard to tell, of course. He's not called Fat Dunc because he looks good in skinny jeans. In his favour, he's still not entirely grey, the only hint being a streak that runs subtly through his full beard on the right side of his face.

Closer still – and when he sees me, he leers in that way he always has since the day I turned sixteen – is Neil. He insists I call him Uncle Neil, just adding to the creep factor. He wears a black suit that hangs off his frame. As kids, we called him Skeletor, but with old age advancing on him, Neil looks more like one of the undead than ever. The years of drug abuse didn't help his complexion, and even if he's clean now, I don't think he'll ever be able to get rid of the last vestiges of powder that's been stuck in his bloodstream since the mid-'80s.

Right at the back, of course, is Jenny Hanson. Still big, but mostly in the ways that men like. Her clients adore her oversized bouncy breasts, barely contained by the little black dress she's inappropriately squeezed herself into. Jenny went on the game when she turned eighteen, and while she's only a year older than me, she looks like she's been in the life for decades. For a few years, she was Tony's bit of choice. Now he wouldn't touch her with another man's, and she's running her own stable to make ends meet. Most of her girls are drug addicts. She still kicks up ninety per cent of profits to Tony. Hardly what you'd expect of the girl who kicked every arse she met while at school. But I'm beginning to wonder if Mum didn't have a point when she said that, deep down, Jenny was scared.

I never understood what she meant when she said that, not really. Figured mum was just saying any old rubbish to make me feel better. But the older you get, the more you realise that no-one is who you think they are, or who they want you to think they are.

All these faces, they're looking right at me. And they're asking the same question: what are you doing here?

It's a good question. When I left, I did so with the dramatic force of the righteous. Telling myself I wasn't like the rest of the family, that all of this wasn't who I am. Tony, high as ever, had left messages on my mobile, telling me that if I ever betrayed the family, he'd kill me.

I never wanted to betray anyone.

Just wanted out.

I almost managed to avoid the service. I could have climbed in the car and driven away, back up to Oban and the little flat I got that overlooked the harbour. Only a few months, and the quiet life is already more real to me than anything else I've ever known.

I had almost believed I had that rarest of chances: a new start.

The organ cranks into life. People stay seated, waiting for that invisible cue to stand. I smooth down my dress, look at my shoes. People shift around me. I stand. Throughout the hymn – solemn, slow – I occasionally open and close my mouth, wonder how everyone knows the words to this dirge. Sounds the same to me as almost every other hymn ever written.

I keep looking around. Wondering where he is. If he's even going to show his face. Did they tell him I'd be coming?

Wouldn't be a Scobie family gathering without some kind of drama, right?

When the music finally finishes, it's replaced by the sniffs of people who can't control themselves. Reflexively I wipe at my eyes, realise that I've been crying as well.

He was a psychopath, my cousin. Same as all of them, really.

But in the end he was family. And you can run away all you like, but it's always going to be family that brings you back. One way or another.

John

I can't go to the service.

Not if she's going to be there. I'm a bastard – both in and out of cover – but I'm not that much of a bastard. Besides, being in there, knowing that's not his corpse in the coffin, that gives me more time to plan.

Or panic.

Because I'm past plans. Past ideas. I'm spinning my wheels until something happens. About as useless as asking God for help, in my experience. You get stuck in the mud, you only get out through your own efforts.

So I do what any sensible west coaster does when life conspires against them: head for the pub.

This place, it's quiet and anonymous. The beer is standard: straight up choice of McEwans or Tennents, with anything else getting you branded a wee poofter, and likely a kicking outside to boot. But long as you drink your pint in peace, the locals do little more than give you the hairy eyeball.

I drink in peace. Keep my phone on the table.

Watching. Waiting.

When it buzzes, the back of my neck prickles. Someone walking over my grave? Maybe. I check the message. Sure enough, it's Tony.

She's here.

Of course she is. I'm glad, too. Maybe I don't feel it consciously, but there's a smile on my face.

'Message from your girl?'

What did I say about drinking my pint in peace?

I look up. The man standing at the table sways and gives me a grin designed to show off black and yellow teeth. His hair is grey, and his face marked with right stubble that looks capable of blunting any razor brave enough to get close. He says again, as though I didn't hear him the first time: 'Message from your girl?'

I shake my head.

'Your boy?' This time, his voice takes on an edge.

Give me strength.

'Just piss off,' I say.

'You don't look like a poof.'

I resist the urge to respond.

'Doesn't mean anything.'

From friend to foe in less than two seconds. This guy, I doubt it's an unusual occurrence.

'Got nothing to say?'

'Not to you.' He chews on that for a moment. But he still doesn't leave.

'I just want to have my drink in peace.'

'Poof.'

He leans on the table, now gets right in my face. Trying to use the word like a closed fist. 'Poof.'

It's not the insinuation. Like I give a monkeys what he thinks of my sexuality. But something in me finally snaps. I reach up and wrap my hands round his head. The move feels almost casual, but it's too quick for him to react. I tug him down, sharpish, bounce his face off the top of the table and let go.

He slides off the table, onto the floor.

I stand up.

The fat man who's been standing behind the bar all this time says, 'Aw, come on, pal!' but doesn't do anything else. I look at him, and he holds up his hands in surrender. Working in this place, he knows there's no point calling the police. This kind of thing, it's predictable as the weather and every bit as dull. He just goes back

33

to standing behind the bar, rearranging the glasses, keeping one eye on the telly. Like nothing happened.

I look at the old guy on the floor. He's moaning and rolling.

I spit on him.

Walk out.

The air is sharp. The kind of slap in the face that sobers you up. Clarity overtakes me. I realises what I've done.

Catch sight of myself in the pub window. A pale reflection. Washed out. Almost unreal. I have this expression on my face, a kind of sneering, hate-filled twisting of my features. My lips pulled back in a snarl, my eyes lit up with the kind of adrenaline-rush I recognise from dealing with Anthony Scobie.

It's like looking at the ghost of a stranger. I take two steps back, suddenly breathless.

Who am I? The cop or the criminal? Right now I'm stuck in limbo between the two. Need to figure out who I am, what I do next.

Time is running out, after all.

Kat

As we leave, they play a Johnny Cash spiritual over the speakers. Hardly orthodox, but we're modern Catholics. Besides, Ray liked Johnny. Listened to him a lot. Wore down his father's old records he listened to them so often.

But it was the young, rebellious Johnny, or the old, broken-down one that got Ray going. Not the middle-aged, middle-of-the-road, religious sap infused stuff they're piping out just now.

Could be worse, I suppose. They could be playing Fat Elvis.

Maybe he'd have cracked a smile at that.

If he ever smiled.

Out the back of the church, we do the line-up. I hug Anthony briefly. Get this urgent sensation down my spine that makes me break the embrace too quick.

Looking into his eyes, I see he's high.

Not a surprise. It's his coping mechanism. With life in general. The day Tony's not high or thinking about getting high is the day you know there's something seriously wrong with the world.

When I embrace Uncle Derek, he squeezes me tight, whispers in my ear, 'I'm sorry, love,' like the loss is mine, somehow.

And that's when I lose it.

• • •

Seventeen years old.

In my bedroom, hating all men.

At least, all boys.

The first betrayal is always the worst. Colours your view of relationships forever. Sets a patter for the way that you react to all the inevitable betrayals that will follow it.

His name was Andy Cook. A year above me, with an arse that looked great in jeans. And the kind of smile that suggested the very safe kind of naughtiness you need when you're seventeen.

He had been my first, too. The first to make me wonder what all the fuss was about. But I figured you probably got better with practice.

It was easy to fool yourself into believing in love at that age. Thinking that you probably can't do better, that the first reasonably good-looking boy who comes along with a wink and a smile is probably the one. When all you've found is someone who'll look at you for more than two minutes without nodding off or leering at a girl with breasts like Emily Hendricks'.

Emily Hendricks. The wee trollop. That was who he'd gone with. He made sure he didn't leer at her breasts when I was around, but all the same…

He admitted it when I confronted him. Bold as brass, my grandmother would say.

He told me down the chippy. So what I did was drop my poke, turn and walk away. No screaming. No shouting. I walked back home – over a mile – thinking about nothing, walking on auto-pilot. When I got in the door, Mum was in the kitchen, stuck her head out to ask me how the evening was. 'You're back awfy early.'

I didn't answer, went up to my room. Started crying when the door was shut. And didn't stop. Even when Mum knocked, I didn't stop except to tell her to go away.

Only made things worse.

It was maybe two hours before there was another knock at the door. Again, I yelled at whoever it was to just leave me alone.

But Ray walked right in.

Five years since he saved me from Jenny Hanson. Things were different, but still felt the same.

When Ray came in and sat down on the bed, I hugged him. He stiffened, but then returned the hug. Awkward. His hugs always were. Like he didn't understand them.

We stayed that way a long time. I liked the smell of his after-shave. Made me feel safe, for some reason.

Finally, he let go. 'Your mum's worried.'

I told him what happened.

When I was done, he nodded. Stood up. For all the moments when he could be so nice, there were other times I suspected Ray wasn't much more than a robot mimicking human behaviour. Sometimes I wondered if he understood other people beyond learning the rules for reacting to them.

'That's it?' I asked.

He nodded, left the room. I waited a few minutes before sheep-ishly going downstairs to talk to Mum. In the kitchen, she offered me a glass of wine. I refused, and she laughed. So I took the wine, and she led me into the living room. It's the first time I remember her treating me like an adult. An equal

Mum sat on the couch, legs curled up beneath her. We talked about a lot of things. I think maybe that evening was the one where me and Mum finally became close again, shared experiences of shitty boyfriends making bad mistakes, laughed about men in general. And finally accepted each other as real human beings.

She would be dead two years later.

Looking back, I think maybe that was the night we both knew something was wrong. She got drunk quicker than I'd ever seen her before, and when she tried to go to bed, she seemed too silly, as though her wine had been stronger than mine. She practically fell over the banister when she tried to go to bed, and would have gone right the way over if I hadn't caught her. I would later see a lot more behaviour like that, even when she hadn't been drinking, that cancer slowly destroying her from the inside out, manifesting itself in ways none of us ever expected.

But for that night, she was the mother I wanted. The mother I needed. I'm glad we had some time like that.

'Why'd you keep me out, but let Ray in?'

I tried to pretend I hadn't heard the question. It was that point in the evening where I was pleasantly drunk, but not willing to over-share. But it felt good to be curled up in the big armchair with the telly on in the background, one empty and one open bottle of red on the table.

'Kat? Honey, you listening to me?'

'Yes, Mum.'

'Well?'

I shrugged, resorted to the monosyllabic responses that had been typical of my mid-teenage years. They hadn't quite left me. I still used them in moments of extreme stress or discomfort.

'I'm your mother, Katherine,' she said. But the use of my full name didn't quite seem to hold the power it once did. Even if she'd gone full-on *Katherine-Jane Scobie*, I don't think it would have felt quite so much the skelp on the bum that it used to. 'I want you to be able to...' she stopped, then, and laughed. It wasn't a public laugh, sounded weirdly sad. 'I want to be your friend too. But...I know I was never... My mother and I, we were never really that close. She wanted to be, but I... Oh, honey, you'll know one day.'

'I let Ray in,' I said, choosing my words carefully, like Princess Diana treading through minefields in front of cameras, 'because I thought he could....because he made me feel better before. A long time ago. He helped me, you know?'

'Did he help you now?' Mum sounded sceptical, but I wasn't sure why.

'It was nothing,' I said, remembering now how she used to ask why Jenny Hanson didn't come round for tea any more, as though we had been the best of friends at primary school and not just two oddballs thrown together because there wasn't really anyone else to talk to. 'Just.... I thought maybe he could...'

'Honey, you don't want him to help with this.' Then, she seemed to think about something. 'You didn't ask him to do something, did you?'

'No.'

'Good. Good. Fine. It's just, a man like Ray, he has his own way of doing things. He's not...he's never been like you or me.'

'A girl?'

She hesitated, and then laughed like a drain before starting to fill up our glasses again. I wondered if we'd get into a third bottle. And if I could handle it. I was still sober enough to know that I didn't want my own mum seeing me wrecked.

There are some lines that should never be crossed.

'No, no, that's not what.... Christ, Kat, you're a royal pain in the arse, sometimes. No, I mean...' I worried that she was about to turn serious again. 'I mean that a man like Ray, he's not like… He's... You must have noticed that he's not, I mean in the way he speaks and all, so quiet and serious. He was born with something of a…he's…he's got a…condition. And the way it affected him was he didn't quite feel the world in the same way as other people. He was pretty sick when he was young.'

'Ray?' Hard to believe, the kind of man he was.

'I know, I know! True, though. Had to look out for him constantly, until he was old enough to take care of himself. Gave him something of a violent streak. He didn't always know when he was really hurting people. He didn't understand how they felt.'

It didn't make sense to me at the time, although I knew she wasn't trying to mess with me or anything. She was trying to tell me the truth. But only by hinting around it.

'I'm just saying, the way he helps people isn't the way most of us would. That's all.' She shook her head. 'But we've got more wine, and you say you told him you didn't need his help. So let's drink.'

At her funeral, my uncle Derek would tell me that was her way of changing the subject: 'If she didn't like what you were saying,' he told, smiling at the memories, 'she'd say, 'let's drink.' You never really had a choice.'

It was two days after my little bonding session with Mum when I saw the morning news and inhaled air that sliced through my throat like the wrong side of a Ginsu knife.

I wasn't really listening when the report started, but was dimly aware that a body that had found near Glasgow Green. I glanced at the screen, saw Andy's face. That was when the knife tried to slice me open from the inside out. When I had to gasp for a clean, natural breath.

That was when I realised the truth about Ray; who he was, what he was capable of. The kind of work he really did for my uncle.

• • •

In the bathroom, I look at my face, wonder if anyone will know that I had a little breakdown. It's a funeral, and people don't mind if girls cry, but it matters to me a great deal. I don't like to show weakness.

Where the hell is John? He should be here. His clients shouldn't be more important than this.

I lean forward, check my face the same way I used to for spots. Take a deep breath and straighten up. I look okay.

No. No, I look better than okay. I look stunning. Check the red hair, pale skin and black dress. Classic. The bloodshot eyes only add to the melodramatic beauty.

Could have come straight from central casting: mysterious mourner at the funeral.

It's a sad day when you can't even believe your own delusion.

As I turn to go, someone else comes in.

Jenny Hanson looks worse than me. Says, 'I need to clean up.' All mascara smudge and spot-stress breakout.

'You okay?' I ask her, not really caring, thinking that because this is a funeral I can set aside my personal feelings and reach out to another human in need.

She scowls. 'Get fucked, Lesbo.' Bustles into a cubicle. I turn back to the mirror. Hear snorting noises, know she's not sniffing back the tears.

I'm a failure as a Scobie.

All my mum's fault, of course. She was the black sheep who refused to get involved with any of my uncle's business. He'd been the one who did well for himself, brought the family back from the brink of poverty. But Mum always said that there were other ways of doing what he had done. That he took the easy way.

Didn't stop her from taking gifts, though, from letting him help her. I guess that was when it started, when I realised her hypocrisy.

John was supposed to be my escape. I'd thought he was different from the parade of boys who wanted to get closer to my family rather than just me. I'd thought *here's someone who lives a normal life*. I'd had visions of children and a house in the country. A normal life. A new name. A family forgotten. Sooner or later, my intention had been to use him as an excuse, a means of escape.

'Oh, it's not my fault, but John and I need the space, or he's the one uncomfortable with how you live your lives.'

And then it happened. Of course it did. He told me he was just being polite, reaching out to my relatives. Then I found he was doing work for them. Just little favours, he said. But with my uncle, there's no such thing as little favours.

I could have been like my mother. Turned a blind eye. Accepted my lot in life. She was the one had the excuse, of course. I knew my dad had wanted out. Before he died, I remember hearing him have strong talks about getting away from my uncle and everything he stood for. But Mum was entrenched in the family, even if she paid lip service to escape. I sometimes wonder if that's what really killed dad – the exhaustion of dealing with the Scobies.

Them that asks no questions...

My dad read me that poem when I was a girl. Rudyard Kipling.

It's my only truly solid memory of my dad, really. This presence. This voice: deep, sonorous. Intoning the words as we watch shadows on the wall...

Watch the wall, my darling, as the gentlemen go by.

I don't miss him because I never really knew him. Other than half-remembered, maybe even imagined arguments heard through walls and the sense that here was a man who would give his life to protect his daughter. He died in a traffic accident when I was five. I don't know that I even cried because I didn't understand what his death meant.

Was he as dirty as my uncle? As complicit as my mother?

I look at myself in the bathroom mirror.

Thinking, *what am I doing here? I escaped.* John's betrayal giving me that shove I finally needed, the confidence to cut all ties.

Jenny, in the stall, lets loose a long sigh. I find myself wondering if what she has is from Tony's stash. I think about how she looked when she came in here.

I run the taps, splash my face again and re-apply my makeup.

The mirror. I look better. More human. There's something, at least.

I turn and glance at the locked stall where Jenny's floating away on her little cloud. Consider asking for some. I've never done drugs before, but there's always a first time.

And then I shake my head.

Stupid idea. Best to face the world wide-eyed and sober. More painful. But maybe pain's what you need, sometimes.

John

I still have her picture in my wallet. Passport sized. These days, it's behind my driver's licence, but it's still there.

Stupid, really. Sentimental.

The problem with telling lies is that if you repeat them often enough you start to believe them.

I don't know whether I really did love her or just convinced myself that it was the truth.

When they take me in – and they're going to, one way or the other – I figure the psychiatrist is going to have a field day during debrief.

I'm in the hotel room I booked after covering up Ray's survival. Not a difficult matter to book under a stolen card and assumed ID.

It's a small room, the most basic I could find. The window looks out onto an alley, and while it's central enough, it hardly matches the opulence of the refurbished Central Hotel itself, just a few streets away.

At least there's a TV. Cheap flatscreen with a wonky remote you have hold at a very particular angle before anything happens. I tune in to STV, get crowd shots of the funeral.

'…The Scobie family's solicitors have issued a statement denying that Raymond Scobie's death was connected to any criminal wrongdoing…'

Aye, of course they have. I sit down on the edge of the bed and watch.

I don't listen to what the reporter has to say. She's talking about the family's history of legal difficulties and their ties to some of the city's more colourful history. It's torturous, the way she can't come out and directly say they're the biggest crime family since the Krays. Legal issues and all that.

I look at the assembled. They couldn't get inside the church, of course, but they managed to get some nice angles from across the street.

And then I see her. She's got her back to the camera, but it's her. I'd know her anywhere.

And my heart, clichéd as hearts can be, skips a beat.

· · ·

'You're confident, then?'

She looked at the drink, then at me. Impressed but wary. Who could blame her? Impressed because I knew she drinks Prosecco to the exclusion of almost anything else, wary because why would a stranger know that?

Thing is, I knew almost everything there was to know about Katherine 'Kat' Scobie, including the fact that she always excluded her middle name from official forms and that she'd been considering changing her family name by deed poll.

She hated them that much.

But they loved her.

Go figure.

Some ways, I was jealous. Given my own family. Or lack thereof. But that didn't matter. None of it mattered. All that mattered was that I needed to make her feel she'd found someone she could trust.

'I don't take drinks from strange men.'

I offered my hand. 'John.'

'Just because you have a name doesn't make you not a stranger.'

'We're all strangers,' I said, 'until we're not.'

It made her smile at least.

'And what do you do?'

'It's not going to be a terrifically sexy answer.'

'Truth can be sexy.'

'An accountant.'

'Then again.' But I still got a smile.

And it was enough.

• • •

I still have her number stored on my phone's memory. I think of her when I wake up in the morning. I have that photo hidden under my driver's license.

She was supposed to be a means to an end. But now?

God only knows.

Six months since she left. I figured that the end of our relationship would also be the end of my operation: after all, she was the reason that Derek Scobie trusted me. But the odd thing was that once she announced her intention to cut all family ties, I was brought in deeper than I ever expected. Filling a void, maybe? I was their last connection to her, perhaps.

Check out McFreud here. Like I have any special understanding of the motivations of the criminal mind. I barely understand why I do anything, or at least I try not to think too deeply about it. This was one of the reasons Crawford picked me for the job: 'Undercover work means believing everything you do. You analyse whether your behaviour is correct, they'll catch you out.'

Crawford had been happy with my appointment. I'd been uncertain.

And then things went to hell.

When the report on the TV finishes, I look at her number. I've considered calling her a number of times since she left, but I don't even know that she kept the number. The idea was that she just cut all ties with her family, with what she called the 'cancer' of Derek Scobie's influence.

She just wanted to be normal.

Who could blame her?

My finger hovers over the 'call' button. But I back out of the menu, put the phone away.

She's back for her cousin's funeral. She deserves the chance to mourn like a normal person.

Chances are that Ray Scobie's actually dead, anyway. This is a real funeral. The cadaver isn't his, of course – took me a while to arrange that particular bit of subterfuge – but he's been missing since his escape from hospital for almost a week now. His injuries, he has to be dead. He's tough, but he's not immortal.

Besides, he would have made a play. I'm sure of it.

My phone buzzes.

Anthony:

Come 2 the Crow.

I hesitate and then reply: *Don't want 2 upset her.*

Takes less than thirty seconds for the reply to crack back: *Pussy.*

I smile and shake my head. Figure I'm in this deep. I want to redeem myself, I need to give Crawford something when he finally hauls my arse in. Maybe the wake's the place to do it. Find the cracks. Expose the truth.

Redeem myself.

At least in part.

Kat

'Tell me the truth, he cheat on, your boyfriend?'

'Fiancé.' Before correcting myself, quickly: 'Ex-fiancé.'

Neil, in the driver's seat, smirks. Caresses the gearstick. The innuendo makes *Carry On* films look subtle. It's hard to tell if he really is trying it on. Acting like a filthy bugger is simply a habit. He suffers from Tourette's of the letch.

My family have always had such good taste in friends.

'Your ex-fiancé,' he says, with uncomfortable emphasis, and again that smirk. 'But you didn't answer the question.'

'No,' I say. 'He didn't cheat on me.'

I think about slapping him. Would feel good. When he talks to me, he talks to my chest and legs, never to my face. Pretty much standard behaviour for him around any woman below thirty.

But Neil is family. Not blood. But he's been around forever. Adopted, if you like.

Like Fat Dunc. And Pete and Wayne.

The Scobies welcome you. They understand about being judged. Accept you as you are. Unless you're a copper. Or a narc. Over the years, others were welcomed in. Family by association, not blood. Some were by marriage, like my dad. Others simply by the good grace of Uncle Derek.

And despite everything I said when I left, all of them act like I never even left. There's something admirable in that, I suppose. I understand the seduction, maybe, the way that they can make you feel like you belong.

I watch the old roads go past. We drive deeper into the city, into Scobie family history and legend. Slipping away from the opulence of the Newlands and back to a reminder of who we were and where we came from. The real South Side, I suppose.

I think about Ray. The man I knew. The rumours I heard. I try to work out the reasons someone would plant a bomb in his car.

I think about the rumours. The veiled warnings Mum made when I confided in him what my bastard of an ex had done to me. About the look that Ray would get sometimes in other people's company, like he was trying so hard to fit in with everyone.

He was at once a lost child and a dangerous animal. I'd always liked him, and even knowing what he did for my uncle, there's something in me wants to believe he had another side; a human side.

Oh, Ray, what did you do?

Who were you?

Really?

John

Like a teenage boy habitually texting his crush, Anthony sends me continuous updates of the day's proceedings and his father's growing anger at me.

Big bacon gathering outside the church – fuck tha police!

I keep telling Dad you're missing this bcoz of Kat. He's still pissed off.

Of course Derek Scobie's hacked off. He ordered the death of his eldest son and he's still not sure he did the right thing.

The evidence was there, though. Told a story anyone would find hard to deny. And Christ knows I tried.

They'd called me in as a third party. Not that I knew it when Tony picked me up, not saying a word about what was happening, got me high in the car on the way over. That was his way of checking that he could trust me, nothing to do with his dad, who simply asked for Tony to pick me up.

Still don't know if Scobie Senior knew about this wee quirk of his son's, or if it was something he just had to overlook. Derek had to know that Tony was off his trolley, but I was different. He still looked at me as a citizen, someone easing his way into their world, not born to it. One of the reasons Derek trusted – *trusts* – me is because I know to stay clean, or at least give the appearance of it.

The meeting had been a strained and terrifying affair. Made worse by my own paranoia and the fact that no-one present wanted to admit what they were really thinking.

• • •

My first thought, walking into the garage near the Arches on Midland Road, was that I was a dead man. This was it. I had reached the end. There were only two ways my assignment would end. Either the bosses pulled me, or the Scobies emptied out the inside of my skull.

I'd been asked to pull the operation three hours earlier. Said

I just needed more time. Of course, I should have known things would go straight to shit.

I figured my time was due. Just hoped they'd make it fast.

The one thing I couldn't figure: how they worked me out. Which was why I wasn't begging on my knees or spilling the whole story, just keeping quiet as possible, remaining in character, hoping against hope I could find a way to stay alive, wriggle my way out from under their suspicion.

One of the reasons I'd been chosen for the operation was that there would be no-one to miss me if things went sour. No kids. No wife. No siblings. No parents. No real friends, either. I wasn't the type to go down the boozer on a Saturday afternoon and catch up with the lads. And any girls I knew didn't hang around for long, often sensing something in me they didn't want to know.

So, aye, if things went wrong, then I'd be the only one who really suffered.

Cynical? Maybe.

Just outside the garage, my heart slapped out its own disjointed beat; a cocaine-fuelled jazz-nut who'd lost any sense of the music and was finding his own time, his own rhythm.

'You know what we do.'

Derek Scobie spoke with the kind of gravitas that sends shivers down your spine. Way I felt, I figured it was the same sensation that someone about to be inducted into the Masons experiences.

'You know what we do.'

'I know,' I said.

'You chose me over my niece.'

'I think she's the one who made the choice,' I said. The words out of my mouth before I even thought about them. The cocaine talking, I figured. It was a little odd, this feeling like I was watching myself, unable to really control my actions.

My heart quit the crazy beat. Quit any kind of beat. I thought I might just pitch forward there and then, save them the trouble of killing me.

I should have found a way to refuse the drugs, but Anthony Scobie doesn't let you say no.

Derek Scobie quit pacing. Regarded me for a second with the kind of eyes I imagined were the last thing a mouse might see before it its belly got ripped open. 'You're a good man, John. A good man. Had to be, for my niece to even look at you. I mean, before...' He let that one hang in the air.' But you're no idiot. You know what I do. You've helped me. You've helped,' gesturing around the room, taking in everyone present, 'us.'

Us meaning the old man himself, his youngest son, the slimy fuck Neil and Fat Dunc. The inner circle. The criminal equivalent of King Arthur's round table.

'Where's Ray?'

'Ray's the reason we're here,' said Neil. 'The reason we need to talk to you.'

I got this lump in my throat. Big enough I could have choked. I knew what Ray did. He dealt with unwanted problems. And he wasn't in the room.

Meaning he was...where?

'Just sodding well tell him,' Tony said. 'Put the bollocks out of his misery. To shite with all this clock and dagger, aye?'

No-one bothered to correct him. No-one ever really bothered to correct him about anything.

Derek turned those predator eyes on his youngest son. The old man had come up as an enforcer for bigger, more powerful men. Feared across the city. Although you looked at him now, all you saw was skin and bones. But he had this look, the one that made you stop whatever you were doing, start looking over your shoulder for the Grim Reaper. That was how he looked at me when I came in, and he looked at Tony now. Giving the cocky little bastard no choice but to back down.

The situation defused, Derek turned to look at me again. 'Family is everything. You know that already, son. We've taken you in. Helped you make something of yourself.'

True enough. I'd been a pretty poor pretend accountant. Now I was a pretty poor pretend accountant making thousands through money-laundering for this prick. Kicking back any personal profits to the evidence locker, of course.

Not skimming any off the top for my personal compensation.

No, no, not at all.

In the silence, I wondered if I'd spoken out loud. My thoughts were as distinct as speech. I thought I could hear them echoing around the room. I couldn't keep them in my head. They were escaping.

The drugs.

That cool little observer chuckled to himself while my body went into overhyped fight or flight. The paranoia ramping. The sweat breaking cold on my forehead.

Derek Scobie placed his hands on my shoulders. I thought of Jack Palance in the Michael Keaton *Batman* movie telling Jack Nicholson he's Palance's number one guy.

'Are you in, John? All the way?'

'Family,' I said. 'I didn't have much of one. I look at what Kat walked away from, what you have… She made the wrong decision. Why I stayed, aye? You've… Aye, sure, whatever you need.'

My stomach threatened to escape whichever route was fastest. My skull started to press tight against my brain.

Derek Scobie didn't notice: 'Dunc over there once told me that family wasn't about blood. Maybe he was right. Because it's the blood that betrays you. In the end.'

Anthony stood up, then. Shaking, skin pale, eyes wide. 'Fuck sakes, Dad! Just get to the point!'

'My niece hurt me by walking away, by treating me like I was some kind of monster. That was bad enough. The things she said, about who I was, what I did…to her…to you, even…' He shakes his head. I act like I don't understand, trying not to remember the piercing stab wounds that had been Kat's final conversation with me.

Derek Scobie takes a deep breath. He looks at me. Right in the eyes. 'But then, you see, my son – my own son – turned out to be a fucking traitor.'

Not Anthony.

No, not him. Not the drugged-up fuckbag. Not the one you would have expected to try and sell out his father for his own personal gain.

No, he was talking about the quiet, dependable killer. The number-one son. The giant who did whatever he was told. Who had never shown any signs of dissent, whose own motives were always hidden.

Ray. The implacable bastard had sold out. Sided with Buchan. Betrayed his family.

The worst sin. At least in the eyes of Derek Scobie.

You can screw over a friend. You can cheat a lover. But you don't betray blood.

Not if you're a Scobie.

Those were the rules. And Ray, so Derek believed, was the one who finally broke them. Broke the family.

Kat

We're barely inside the Crow and Claw when it starts.

The headache of family reunions. The false bonhomie, the enforced sense that Uncle Derek's dictates about the closeness of family were just built into us by virtue of our genes.

I remember when I was a kid, Mean Jean getting 'tired and emotional' at a cousin's wedding, walking from group to group, chanting, 'the family's all together!' like it was the most miraculous thing in the world. To her, maybe it was. To me, it seemed like the family was always together. The Scobies were like the Alcatraz of relations: there was no escape.

The Scobie clan is a sprawling mass, held together by blood and mostly common interests. Not all of us are crooks. But most of us skirt a fine line. Figuring it worked for Derek, and anything we do will never be half as risky.

But here's the important thing: we never ever rat on our own.

That's the rule. The particular, golden one. You can be straight-up as you like, but you can't talk to the police. Family is more important than anything else. Uncle Derek says so, and Uncle Derek is God.

It felt good to escape all that nonsense. Up in Oban, looking out at the harbour from my flat, it was so easy to pretend that my family were dead, that they never existed, that they had no hold.

I stick by the car for a while, nauseous and trembling. Watching the bar across the road, and all the people milling on the pavement and in the door.

The Crow and Claw.

Where it all began. Uncle Derek's first legitimate business, still his in all but title deed. A crappy little bar near Govanhill, what you'd call spit and sawdust, although that might seem a little pretentious. It's the kind of bar where you drink only if you know someone else who drinks there.

I haven't been here in years. But it's like a magnet for the family. Every funeral, christening, wedding, whatever, we wind up back here getting pissed and being watched by the local coppers, who have a station just two streets away.

I'm willing people not to come near me. If someone tries to hug me, then I don't know what I'll do.

Vomit, probably.

Had an old boyfriend did that first time he met Uncle Derek. Shook the old man's hand, vomited on his shoes.

Mean Jean's making a beeline. Stumbling across the road, nearly collapsing on those heels she insisted on wearing. I don't get how they support her well-compacted weight.

I plaster a smile. My cheeks ache from the effort.

She says, 'Oh, it's a terrible shame, love.'

'Aye, Jean, it is.'

She doesn't hug me, but does the air kiss instead, still thinking that I'm some kind of big city sophisticate because I lived in the West End for a few years. The strength of her perfume nearly knocks me down. She must have doused herself in it. Light a match, she'd go right up.

Like Ray.

Oh, aye. This is the perfect time to think of jokes like that.

'Should get a swally down you,' Jean says. 'Make you feel better.' Because it works so well for her.

I nod, and say, 'In a minute. I… The fresh air, you know?'

'Of course. I know, love.' She looks round. Her eyes are wide, and her mascara is smudged just right so you know she's been crying. 'Oh, it was such a beautiful. And he's… Oh, the choices these lads make. It's…oh, it's death after death after death…'

She's heading for a public meltdown. Anyone else, I'd stay and offer them some support. Mean Jean, I just want to get as far away as possible.

No time for excuses, I just walk right up to the front door of the club. Inside, I can hear glasses clinking and people talking.

Deep breath.

I wonder if John's here. I hope he's the man I remember, at least. That man would have the decency to make his excuses. Because I know Tony's told him I'm here. My cousin would delight in the potential drama.

John, please, I think, *just stay away. Don't make today any harder than it has to be.*

Someone bumps into me. I apologise. They hug me, sobbing. I don't even know their name, just try and figure out if they're a man or woman and who they might be related to.

The Crow and Claw swallows me. Calling me home. With the rest of the family.

John

I pull up outside the Crow and Claw. Turn off the engine. There are a few people I recognise smoking outside. The wake is in full swing. Can't fault a Catholic family when they remember the dead. They do it in style.

Absolution covers many sins.

I get out of the car, put on my face, walk inside. A few of the guys nod. Looking uncomfortable.

Old joke:

What do you a call a Scobie in a suit?

The defendant.

I'd rather be walking in with Kat, here as her fiancé, not as the bloody cuckoo in the nest. But that ship sailed long ago.

Now I have to keep my eye on the prize.

Retain some measure of dignity.

I'm looking for redemption here. Maybe all that Catholic guilt has rubbed off on me after all.

One of those puffing away out front is a big, Polish lad named Piotr. Second generation, thick accent inherited from his parents and shot through with a nasal Glaswegian twang. No-one pronounces his name correctly, so they just call him Pete. He doesn't seem to mind. He's a chain smoker, wears ill-fitting shell suits in migraine-inducing neon. But today he's all trussed in up in a black suit that's just a little too tight around that barrel chest. A thin black tie threatens to choke him, a noose around his neck.

'John,' he says, gives me a wink.

I feel like he can see me for what I really am.

And who is that? The cover? The man in the mirror? Or someone else?

Hold it together, man.

'Pete,' I say, keeping it cool, shrugging the paranoia. 'Where's Wayne?'

'Probably eyeing up some local talent,' Pete says, and laughs.

'Such as you fucking get here.'

They make an unlikely couple, Pete and Wayne, and you'd expect them to be ostracised for their private lives, but they're two of Scobie Sr's best enforcers. They act easy going and matey, but give them a chance and they'll happily break your legs. They're not subtle. They get the job done. But you'd still rather have them show up at your door than Ray.

Maybe that's why so many people are looking relaxed this evening. His death demands mourning, but I figure a lot of people are relieved. A lot of people know they're going to wake up alive tomorrow morning.

Inside the pub, the chatter of the assembled hits me, staggers me back on my heels. I take a deep breath. Like a drowning man gasping before his head goes under for the last time.

I'm trapped.

I fight to the bar, order a Guinness. Drink of choice for the evening, by the looks of it. Sure, blending in. It's what I do.

A hand claps my shoulder. The fingers sausage-slimy. A weight behind them, so it's hard to tell if the contact's a greeting or just Fat Dunc's way of trying to stay upright.

'Hoping I'd catch you before I leave.'

'Not staying to the bitter end?'

Fat Dunc's drunk. Bloodshot eyes. Skin an unhealthy shade of grey. Makes me want to ask around, check if anyone has a set of defibrillators.

He says, 'It's been a bugger of a week.'

I nod.

'Still can't believe it,' he says. 'What we did.'

Is anyone listening to this? Dunc's not just drunk, he's plastered. Well and truly. That shoulder plant really was about staying upright.

Loose lips sink ships? We're already on board the bloody *Titanic*.

'Dunc, remember where you are.' Meaning, there are civilians here.

He looks up, as though seeing the inside of the Crow for the first time. 'Sod it,' he says. 'Soon enough it's not going to matter. Right? I wanted out. I got out. Except you never really get out. The things I've done…'

I used to work under a shift sergeant who talked in clichés the whole time. The uniforms would take bets on how many he'd spout during the morning meeting. His favourite was the old, *if life gives you lemons, you make lemonade.*

Fat Dunc was one sodding big bag of lemons. But on the plus side, he could probably make a shitload of lemonade. After all, he knew all the dirty little secrets. Even if he was finding it harder and harder to live with them.

He and Derek Scobie had their differences, down the years. Dunc had pulled back on his involvement in the business as the noughties progressed, although he still acted as advisor and confidant. His days as muscle were long gone, but his name still carried some weight. And his opinions continued to hold some sway with Derek.

If I could turn him, maybe there was a way to save my own skin. Make up for all my stupid mistakes.

I say, 'That's dangerous talk.' Confidential. I'm his friend. Looking out for his best interests.

Dunc leans in close. Booze breath strong enough to melt my nostrils. He started long before the wake. Was probably already pissed at the church. 'I'll show you dangerous, son, if you keep pushing. Think you're a big-time gangster now? You're a joke. A pathetic indulgence of the old man's. Get the fuck out before this mess gets you killed. You've had your fun. But you're just a wee boy playing games he doesn't understand. A fucking tourist in our world. Everyone knows it.'

'I'm not playing,' I say, aware instantly that I sound as sulky as the wee boy he was just describing. My heart thump-thumps. Has he figured me out? Has his drunken state allowed him to see more clearly than anyone else here?

He snorts, pulls back. Whirls on his feet, avoids toppling like a rotted oak, and makes his not-so-merry way through the assembled.

I watch him go, think about what he said. Is he just pissed? Do I have a chance of getting to him? He used to be Scobie Sr's most trusted adviser, before Neil slithered his way into the heart of the operation. Maybe I can convince him that turning grass is in everyone's best interests; a way to save the old man from his worst instincts.

Or maybe Dunc's just pissed and talking out of turn, while I'm looking for any solution I can to my own problems.

What happens when Ray's body is found? When everyone figures the deception I played?

It's going to happen eventually. The young doctor can't go on thinking that he's assisting a police investigation. He's naïve, but surely not stupid. And the fake paper trail? An idiot could see through it if they bothered to look.

I was just buying time to sort out my own mistakes.

Sure, I'm running away from them all. But not before I make one final gesture to show how truly sorry I am for everything, how I'm still dedicated to the cause.

Tonight, I turn over one viable witness to Crawford and Burke. I give them the key to taking down the Scobie family.

And then I scarper.

I'm about to order when I hear another voice nearby. I look up. See her ordering a white wine. She hasn't clocked me yet. Of course she hasn't. She'll be praying I'm not here. She'll be thinking maybe I did the decent thing and stayed away.

Decent?

One thing I know: my cover's far from decent.

So I say, 'How're you holding up?' Not a tremor in my voice. The cover so practiced and natural that the observer at the back of my mind can't help but chuckle.

She turns and stares at me. I can see it in her eyes, the hatred and the betrayal. The disbelief, too. She can't believe I'd have the balls to just ask her how she's doing, like nothing happened between us, like she never told me where to go stick all that cash I was making doing odd jobs for her uncle.

She shakes her head, and I'm not sure what the gesture means. She finally just sighs and says, 'It's a funeral.' Pure statement. I nod.

'I had to drive Neil over.' She knows she has to say something.

'Talk about making a bad day worse.'

It gets a laugh at least. Although she cuts off almost immediately.

I swivel, catch the bartender, ask for, 'Anything but a Chardonnay.'

She says, 'Don't.'

'It's not a move.'

'What is it, then?'

'An apology. Too little, too late, I know.'

I feel bad. She won't believe that, but I do. The worst thing about this whole affair, this whole screw-up, has been having to hurt her. Early on, I would have said it was part of the gig. Now, feeling the way I do, it's the only thing that still makes me feel anything. Even if that feeling is little more than shame.

'I was just talking to Dunc,' I say, by way of keeping the conversation going.

'He's pissed.'

'As a fart.'

I wonder what else he's been saying. And who he's been saying it to. My opportunity is close, I know.

'Oh, he'll be fine. Just dealing with it in his own way.' But she doesn't look as sure as she sounds, and I wonder if she has the same suspicions as me about the old bugger's loyalty to his old friends. Whether he's finally reached breaking point with the life.

He wouldn't be the first. Loyalty is tough to keep in the life.

Kat says, 'He told me to leave. Like, early. Think I might take his advice.'

'He say why?'

'He said the evening wouldn't end well. I told him that wakes seldom do.'

'Especially in this family?'

Around us people talk and laugh and share stories that may or may not have anything to do with the deceased. Kat says, 'They chose this life, you know. All of them. They all know that they could die. Even Uncle Derek.'

I laugh. No humour. 'He'll go on forever.'

'They said that about the Queen Mother.'

'Death wasn't afraid of her.'

'I just... I can't believe Ray is...' she doesn't finish the sentence.

I can't look at her.

She says, 'I need to go'

I'm still scanning the assembled, thinking about how many years combined this group would do if the police were to bust them all right now. My brain can't focus on two things at once. Maybe she thinks I'm as uncomfortable with our reunion as she is. Maybe she doesn't care.

Wayne comes up beside me, tenner in hand, ready for another round. Smaller than Pete, he looks more comfortable in his dark brown suit. His standard issue funeral-black tie is loosened just enough to give the impression that he's relaxing into the late after-noon. He sees me, says, 'She still not wanting to talk to you?'

'Aye.'

'She's a tough cookie. She'll be okay. Give her time, all right?'

I nod, thinking that it's insane, me taking advice from a man who makes his money beating the shite out of drug addicts and wasters. Hardly the measure of what you'd call sympathy. And yet here he is, giving me advice on how to deal with Kat and her grief. And it's making some sense.

All I want is to come clean with Kat. Tell her everything. Ask for forgiveness. She's Catholic, after all. Aren't they taught about the power of forgiveness? Or is that all left up to God?

I wonder where she is.

I scan the crowd. Tell myself not to get impatient. She'll be back if she's ready. Jesus, the day's been tough enough without me adding to it.

Mean Jean's talking to Anthony, and it's strange to see the wee big man about town cowed by the sheer force of his auntie's personality. She's the kind of middle-aged woman who'll give it to you with both barrels whether you deserve it or not. And it only gets worse when she's had a few. Which she surely has. That poorly dyed hair of hers rises up like a reanimated corpse when she's drunk, and right now it's reaching for the stars and making me think of the bloodied hand that bursts out of the ground at the end of *Carrie*.

I hunker down at the bar, nurse what's left of my drink. Try not to make eye contact with anyone.

And that's when I hear the gunshots.

That's when the screaming starts.

Kat

I want to be at home.

Curled on the sofa. Watching *Downton*. Or *Midsomer Murders*. Something so patently, ludicrously unreal that it means I don't have to think about Ray. Or any of my family.

The funeral was fine. Necessary. Something we all needed to go through. It's the wake that's going to destroy me: all the Scobies – and all those who want to be Scobies – gathered in the same place at the same time, drinks flowing freely with memories, anecdotes and stories.

Oh, dear God. The stories. Always the same old anecdotes told in the same old way by the same old people before someone dis-agrees about an unimportant detail. And the first punch of the evening gets thrown.

Which is why I need to get out of the bar. Why I've locked myself in this cubicle. I'd rather be anywhere than in the Crow. But the obligations are engraved too deep, so the best I can do is a momentary escape to the loo and a deep, cleansing series of breaths to clean out the inside of my head.

All that, and John too.

I couldn't have lasted another minute. Had this tight feeling in my chest, and my head was too hot. My eyes were not quite watering, but they could have been persuaded.

Delayed grief? Righteous anger? Outside the church I'd found myself confiding in Pete – big, camp teddy bear that he is – about how much Ray meant to me. He was more than my cousin. He was, in my head, an idea. A representation of…something I could never quite put into words.

Safety, I suppose. I always felt safe around Ray. He wouldn't let anything bad happen.

Alone, in the cubicle, I get this odd gasping sensation. Can't hold it in. Blink a few times and then let it out. Cry hard enough that my whole body trembles. I'm shaky and uncertain, my throat closing up, each breath coming in odd and uncertain little gasps.

The feeling reminds me of being a child and finding world too big to cope with.

I let it all out.

And then I lean against the cubicle wall, close my eyes, breath in and out. Slow and steady. I'm heavy, head wobbling about, threatening to roll right off my neck if I'm not careful. But I'm fine. A glitch, that's all. I'm entitled. My cousin's dead.

Murdered.

Family members had died before. Stabbings, shootings, plain old assaults. But death by bomb was a new level of madness. He died without seeing a friendly face. So badly burned, they kept the casket closed. No-one saw his face. Not even his father.

The day after it happened, the police came round to the flat to talk to me about what happened. Giving me chat about how they needed to have a word with every member of the deceased's family in a case like this.

But they weren't there to comfort me. Or any other Scobie. They wanted the dirt. Hoping that what had happened would be horrific enough that we'd talk about family business, finally give them what they had been looking for all these years – a way to get my Uncle behind bars.

I drop the toilet lid, sit down again. My head swimming. Maybe I'm not quite ready to go out there again.

I haven't smoked since I was fourteen, when I spent a year and a bit hanging round the toilets at the back of the school, chaining it and laughing at the stark black and white health warnings on the back of the packets. But now I have the urge. As though a cigarette could change everything. Give me the space to figure out what it is that I'm feeling.

I finally manage to stand without feeling dizzy, leave the cubicle and walk over to the sinks. Run cold water, splash it across my face. I put my bag on the sink, pull out my makeup for a touch up. I need more than that, though. The girl who looks back at me could be an extra in some zombie movie with the sunken eyes and the red blood vessels attacking her iris.

A cool breeze whispers on my face, making me look up. There are small, frosted windows above, prised open to keep the fresh air circling. Or at least what passes for fresh air in the alley behind The Crow.

Voices float in with the breeze. Male. Low. Angry.

I try not to listen. Knowing that it's likely drunken posturing; two men getting upset over nothing, braying like lions vying for dominance.

And then:

'Don't fuck with me, Raymond.'

The words are crystal clear. I have no choice but to listen. Hearing my uncle talking to a dead man. To his dead son. Oh, aye. Definitely my uncle. Trying to sound in control.

But it can't be Ray he's talking to.

Unless I'm the one cracking up here.

'Don't fuck with me, son. You know what you did. Know what I fucking well had to do.'

I want to peek out of those half-open frosted panes, see what's happening. But the sinks are too small to clamber on, and I can't risk slipping. Of the top ten embarrassing places to injure yourself, a crappy pub toilet's got to be in the top five.

I head for the rear fire exit. All the action's near the bar. Back here, it's just a long corridor, the store room and the fire exit. The fire door is prised open a couple of inches, maybe to help the air flow – Glaswegian air conditioning. Boxes and crates make for an obstacle course. Maybe health and safety's on holiday.

Surprise, surprise.

As I reach the door, something catches in my chest. A shortness of breath. A sudden sense that I should turn and run. The same feeling you get in a nightmare; no matter what you do, something bad is about to happen. You just don't know what.

I listen for my uncle's voice. I push the fire door right open, step out into the cool, late afternoon air and see him on his knees, looking at the ground. Ashamed? Penitent?

'You fucked with your own. You betrayed us. What did you think was going to happen?'

There's a man standing in front of him. The alley is cramped, and the shadows from the buildings make for a bad light even in mid-afternoon. I can't quite make out his features, but there's something about him that's familiar. He's dressed in a long, grey coat that doesn't quite sit on his frame: maybe a few sizes too big. In fact all his clothes are badly fitted, as though he just ran through a jumble sale, threw on whatever he could find.

I step closer.

He hasn't seen me.

The man is holding a gun to my uncle's head. A handgun with

a black body and dark grey handle. I don't know guns, don't know the model. But it looks fake. Too insignificant to be real.

The man in the too-big coat turns his head.

His face is scarred. Pale skin, red marks criss-crossing here and there, angry and inflamed. His eyes bulge. His appearance is sickeningly plastic. He looks like someone tried to melt his face off.

He's a monster. An approximation of a human being.

But I know him. I know him.

Ray.

His eyes grab me. Don't let go. I stop. Held there by those eyes. By the hate that burns behind them. Not hate directed at me, but a general, all-encompassing hatred of the world. Uncle Derek lifts his head. Looks at me, and I see only sadness in his eyes. Sadness and weakness.

Ray's mouth opens, as though to say something. But he merely croaks. No words, just a strange sound, a short gasp as though there are no words to say what he feels.

His body hums with anger.

I never really believed what people said about him, but seeing him like this... It's more than just the physical deformity that terrifies me, roots me to the spot.

Again, he tries to speak. It's a tremendous effort, as though the same fire that melted his skin also melted his vocal chords.

My uncle takes the opportunity. Throws himself forward, wraps his arms around Ray's waist and forces the bigger man to stagger backwards into the opposite wall. My uncle's not a big man any more, but he has the element of surprise.

Uncle Derek lets go when Ray staggers, rolls away. But the effort's too much. He's not as young as he used to be and when he tries to move, it's painfully slow. His face stretches in agony. He looks at me like I'm the biggest eejit on the face of the planet. 'Get help, you stupid wee bitch!'

My legs move before I think about it. Like someone slapped me back to my senses. I bolt for the fire door, stumble inside The

Crow, fall over the boxes in that cramped hall, draw in a breath to call for help. I'm ready to yell my lungs hoarse.

But I don't get the chance.

The gunshot beats me to it, loud and sudden, echoing down into unbearably painful silence.

I stay where I am. Frozen. I should run, but I can't move. My body shakes. There are tears hanging in my eyes. My breath bursts in and out of my lungs.

A hand lands on my shoulder. Hot breath tickles me ear and my cheek; someone leaning in close.

'Don't,' the voice says. And it's Ray. But it's not him, either. There's a hoarse crack, like someone's taken sandpaper to his voice box. There's something else, too: a kind of threat that I'd never heard from him before. It touches something in the base of my neck, makes me tense. It's primal, this feeling. I want to run away. Hide in a dark corner somewhere, close my eyes and hope that whatever this thing is, it will pass me over and go on its way.

This thing that might be Ray, with its melted face and broken voice, moves his hand from my shoulder, wraps his arm around my chest and pulls me in close so I can feel his plastic skin press against the side of my head. There's an overwhelming stench of sweat, mixed with a sweeter scent I can't identify that makes me think of almonds.

'If you don't...do what I say...,' The Not-Ray says, gently indicating that I should walk forward. I can't move my head, but my eyes look down and I can see that he's holding something in his free hand. There's a block in my brain, and I tell myself that I don't know what it is. 'If you don't...do what I say, I will not hesitate to kill you.'

I say, 'We buried you.'

'No body.'

'There was…. There was a body. But we buried you… We buried you this afternoon.'

Am I going mad? Is this all in my head?

65

'They fuckin… wish.' He speaks in short, hurried bursts, like it's too much effort to say anything in that sandpaper voice. I'm pressed so tight against his chest that I can feel the sharp rise and fall of his chest, the way his lungs seem to vibrate with each breath, as though it's a superhuman effort just to keep oxygen pumping.

We stumble into the main bar, a strange dance, with Ray taking the lead. All the hub-bub of the Scobie wake stops in a slow wave of silence that ripples from one end of the room to the other.

Did they hear the gunshot over their self-involved chatter? Do they have any idea what's happened?

In the back of my mind, over and over, the question runs:

Will he kill me? Will he kill me?

This is Raymond Scobie. Ray. My cousin. The one who saved me from the bullies.

And yet I know he's serious. He will kill me. It wasn't Ray who saved me. It was the code. The family code. We look out for each other. Now that his father tried to kill him, what's to stop him from killing me? From killing all of us?

I scan faces. See John at the bar. He hasn't moved from his seat. Unlike everyone else, he doesn't look too surprised to see Ray. His brow is furrowed with concern, like he's trying to solve a particularly difficult equation. I want to yell at him to do something, but I can't.

I can't do anything except move where Ray indicates.

Not if I want to live.

I am completely aware of the gun that he carries with his free hand.

The silence makes me want to scream.

'Neil? Anthony?' His voice echoes inside my head.

When I was a girl I'd have dreams about voices that tried to tell me what to do. Used to wake up terrified, not entirely sure I had been dreaming. The voices sounded like Ray.

Neil steps forward, hands raised. Says, 'Fucking Lazarus. Looking better than you did this afternoon.'

'Where's my brother?'

No response.

'Where's the fearty…wee prick?' Longer sentences are a struggle. He has to stop in the middle of them, let his lungs draw enough breath to finish.

Ray points the gun right at Neil. Making a point.

A few years back I went to self-defence classes. Came out pretty good. Learned a load of useful moves. How to disarm someone holding a knife. Knock down a man twice my size.

Of course, the first rule was always this:

Avoid getting into trouble in the first place.

Or, as our instructor put it,

If you can: run.

I'm trying to think of something I could do now that it's too late to make a break. There has to be some way of breaking free from Ray's hold. But I remain compliant. Held in place by a primal fear. Petrified like in some childish game of musical statues.

I want to cry. Ashamed that I can't do anything.

But I can't even summon up tears for that.

Ray says, still talking to Neil, 'He run off? That it? Fucking coward. Talks the talk. But…'

'What do you have to talk about?'

'I killed…our father.'

No-one says anything. The silence makes me wonder if they even heard.

Neil breaks the spell: 'You're a dead man. You're going to wish you were in that coffin.'

'No,' says Ray. Simple.

There is a sound like all the air being sucked out of the room. At once quiet and deafeningly loud. Followed by a dull hum that makes my skull shake. My eyes sting. The world turns fuzzy around the edges.

Neil gasps, mouth dropping open, head rolling forwards. Someone's turned off the volume and slowed the action right down. Neil's arms spread out from his body spasmodically, and his jacket starts to crease in increments as his body flops down into itself. As though someone's punched him in the chest with a giant fist. Red stains spread across his white shirt. His tie flaps.

And then he's down. On his knees. He flops backwards. A yoga position I've never seen before. The red continues to soak through his shirt.

Sound bursts back into the world.

Screaming.

Chaos.

I close my eyes tight. My throat goes cheese-grater hoarse before I realise I'm screaming as much as anyone else.

Ray tugs me back. Awkward, like we're in a three-legged race.

I hated the three-legged race at school. The idea of relying on someone else to be in time with me was the kind of thing that made me hyperventilate.

But now I can't afford to just give up and trip my partner, throw the race like I used to do. Because this time my partner has a gun.

He whispers, 'Run and…I will…kill you…,' and I don't know if he's sorry for what he's doing or that I got in his way.

No-one makes a move to follow us. In shock, perhaps.

The dead man resurrected, Neil's corpse on the floor, not moving. I can't be the only one thinking this isn't real.

We edge out the rear of the club into the alley. Ray says, 'You can…drive, can't you?'

'Yes.' But I don't know why he's asking. It's not dawned on me yet, the reason he took me hostage, why he needed a human shield.

'Good,' he helps me step over the corpse of my uncle. I try not to look at him, to pretend that he isn't there. 'Do what…I say… You might…live.' He stops there, and I don't know if it's because it's too painful to speak or because he thinks I get the point.

I shiver like it's the middle of winter. But the air is warm for the time of year, and objectively I know I'm in a kind of delayed shock. The nurse in me is trying to break through, all that training finally meaning something.

The more I try to stop myself from shaking, the worse it gets.

And I think,

He's going to shoot me.

He's going to kill me.

Ray tugs and whirls me round, out onto the street. He wraps his arm around my shoulder, stands beside me. We could be mistaken for lovers eager to get home as the dark draws in.

Is anyone following us?

I wish I knew. I want to look back. But I can't.

He stops beside a dark blue Megane, the kind of car a mid-level professional might drive. Lets go of me for a moment and fishes the leys from his jacket

I should take the chance to run but I don't do anything. Thinking about the expression on Neil's face as he crumpled to the ground.

Shocked. As though he had expected he might be bullet-proof, somehow. The old lech. Probably believed that too.

'Get in,' Ray says.

I clamber in the driver's side. All perfectly normal. Like nothing's wrong. Roy walks calmly round to the other side of the car. As he's opening the door, I hear a loud bang that makes me duck my head. Someone screams. I think it might be me. A second bang, just as loud but less surprising. Ray thumps into the passenger's seat, slams the door. Says, 'Drive.'

'Where?'

'Anywhere. Just…drive.' He still has the gun. He holds it up. His trigger finger snakes. I want to think he doesn't mean it, but that feeling's in the back of my neck again, and I know that when he says he'll kill me, he means it.

This isn't the Ray I thought I knew. The fire, the explosion, whatever, it didn't just melt away his skin, it melted away his mask.

Underneath, he's a monster. A killer.

Pulling away from the kerb, I glance in the rear view. See John maybe twenty metres behind us, running, feet pounding the gravel path.

I think again about Neil. About my father.

Get us out of there as fast as possible.

John

Three minutes earlier

A second shot.

Definitely gunfire.

Everyone's quiet. The moment stretches. No-one makes eye contact.

Someone laughs and says, 'It's a bastard car backfiring!' A good laugh ripples. The conversation resumes.

We're all paranoid. Jumpy. What does that say?

I'm about to get up when the conversation quiets again, a Mexican wave of silence running from the rear of the bar all the way to the front door.

I look up. See Kat. Then see the man standing behind her, one arm wrapped around her upper body to hold her close.

Jesus Christ, it's Ray. Looking worse – if that's possible – than he did in hospital. Unsteady, but only a minor tremble. Most people in the room probably don't notice.

That he's standing at all is a miracle.

I try not to look at Kat, find a rage building up in my chest. The kind of rage that breaks free, makes you do stupid things. The kind of rage that gets you killed.

So I suppress it as best I can. Focus on other details. Like Ray's free hand. The one holding the gun. Looks like a Glock 17 from where I am. But what does that matter? All guns serve the same purpose. What difference does it make that it's Austrian?

Look at Ray's posture, the way he's holding Kat, leaning on her just a bit too heavy. Like she's a crutch. Maybe a defensive move to make himself less of a target. Or something's seriously wrong.

The doctor said Ray can't feel pain. Doesn't mean he won't know when something's wrong. Like those videos the doc mentioned of kids with broken legs, walking funny and unable to work out why because the signals weren't there to tell them that something was wrong. But Ray's not a kid, he's a grown man. He can put two and two together. He's smart. A predator. Just look into his eyes, you know what he's capable of.

Kat looks right at me. No looking away now. I can't avoid this.

So here's the question: can I do something? Play the hero?

It would be a bloody stupid move. Because Ray will kill her. And me. And anyone who gets in his way.

Why's he here?

Oh, it's obvious, isn't it? He tried to tell me in the hospital, but I ignored what he was saying, believed it to be posturing – real hard-nut stuff, even if that wasn't his style.

Ray makes like he's checking out the room, but what he actually does is make eye contact with me.

Like we share something. A guilty secret.

So I stay still.

Neil challenges him first. This is what Ray wants. He's after Neil. And Anthony. Listen to the way he bellowed his brother's name.

What else does he want?

I know the answer to that without him saying anything.

Me.

Neil.

Anthony.

Derek is missing. Ray doesn't roar his name. Why not?

Neil makes threats. Ray says that he killed the old man.

The whole time, Kat says nothing.

Everything falls into place.

At the hospital, I tried to use the betrayal to turn Ray against his family. But he'd refused. I thought at the time it was out of the stubborn Scobie loyalty. That he was refusing to believe what really happened.

Truth was, he didn't want the kind of revenge that I was offering.

Rolling over, playing bitch for an undercover pig like me? Like fuck was that revenge. His style of retribution was direct. More than anything the justice system could offer. I'd be lying if I said I didn't admire him in some way.

He's still standing.

Not just that he can't feel the pain. He's driven by his desire to confront the men who tried to kill him.

I have to be on that list. But he's leaving me alone for now.

Why?

I sit at the bar like a lemon, utterly powerless. There are maybe forty or fifty people squeezed in the Crow. We keep perfectly still. Like we're watching a film. Long as we don't move, don't say anything, it means that none of this is real.

Ray asks about Anthony.

I haven't seen the little arsewipe in about twenty minutes, maybe more. Did he know something was up? Or just get lucky? Story of his life. The prick should have been killed or slammed up a long time ago, but he's still parading around like king cock of the walk.

Ray and Neil posture. Sizing each other up. A nature documentary, two alpha males trying to force each other to back down.

But it's always going to be Ray who wins this pissing contest. Neil's just a slimy fuck with an inflated ego and an overactive, self-activated sex drive.

That's why it's inevitable when Ray simply shoots the bollocks in the chest. Although people still make shocked noises.

Neil collapses. I don't see his face, but I imagine he's surprised.

No-one moves. Except Ray. He backs up. Takes Kat with him.

Her eyes are wide. She scans the room. Maybe looking for me. Wanting me to meet her gaze, reassure her that everything's going to be okay.

But Neil's death has got me moving. Round the edge of the bar, slow and low. Steady. Making sure Ray doesn't see me.

What's my plan?

Christ knows, but I can't just sit there.

I'm too slow. They're out the rear exit before I get anywhere. I bolt it past boxes and crates that threaten to trip me. When I get outside into the alley, he's gone. Back in the bar, someone hits the play button. There's screaming. Chaos. Panic.

I think about Kipling.

If you can keep your head while all around are losing theirs...

There's a Kipling poem Kat's dad used to read to her. She told me about it once. I have this urge to recall it, but I don't know why.

Out the rear door, the harsh October air assaults my lungs. I gasp. Hesitate. Try to see which way Ray and Kat have gone.

Someone's standing next to me. Low-level thug, name of Michael, wears short-sleeved shirts, has this intricate tattoo round his forearm he likes to show off.

'You see what happened?'

'Madness,' I say.

'Where's the old man?'

'You heard Ray.'

'He can't have killed him. His own father?'

And that's when we spot the body. Abandoned on grey concrete. Arms and legs at awkward angles. Not that the old man cares about comfort any more.

Sod it. Don't let it distract you. Step over his body, let Michael make useless attempts to check for a pulse. Let him flop those arms and legs about to get the corpse into the recovery position. Let him check the airways.

There's no point. I know it. I feel it.

Out the alley, on the street, I spot them. Maybe two or three hundred yards ahead of me. Walking quick, but keeping a low profile. There's a few citizens out dog walking in the early evening.

Ray's smart enough to know that the last thing you do when leaving a crime scene is draw attention to yourself.

I don't give a toss. Run fast. Draw that attention. To shite with it.

But they've got a good lead. I'm close when Ray hustles Kat into a dark blue Megane – a fucking family car, the most ordinary vehicle he could have found. Perfect camouflage.

I stop running. My lungs start to freeze. I can't stand up straight. Can't do it. I can't save her.

Vomit threatens.

Michael's beside me. 'You okay?' I nod.

Michael stays where he is. He raises his arm. He's got a Browning. Army issue. Takes him a moment or two to flip the safety. That's why I know he's already too late. Still, I sidestep and cover my ears as he pulls the trigger. Two shots. But he doesn't hit anything that I can see.

The last thing I notice when I raise my head and watch the Megane peel off down the road is that Kat is driving. And I have to wonder what that means. If it means anything at all.

Three

And When I Die

1615 – 2043

Kat

We pull into the multi-level off Jamaica Street. Driving through the city centre, rush hour getting on, we blended in nicely. The car could have belonged to any suburban couple driving home from work. Long as no-one looked in the windows too closely, saw the face of the man they would have presumed to be my husband.

I kept my driving calm and under control. Focussed on the road, on the destination. I could almost forget witnessing the murder of two men.

I pull into a bay on the third level. Kill the engine. Look out the windscreen, see across the street outside to the buildings opposite, shops and offices closing for the day. When I turn the engine off, a strange silence spreads. Oppressive. Unsettling.

Beside me, Ray stretches, like he's yawning. As though all this has just been a long day, and now all he wants to do is sleep. But there's something in the way he moves, the way his face screws up that tells me he's not tired.

He's been through a lot in the last few weeks, and I'm amazed given the degree of burns across his body that he can walk, never mind kill two people in cold blood

People.

Like I don't know who they are.

But I don't want to think about it.

Maybe he senses the unasked question. Or he's talking to himself. 'They tried to kill me.'

'Who did?'

'The fuck…d'you think?' Like he's just realised I'm there.

I can't say anything. Don't want to say anything. Because that might somehow make all of this real. And I want it to be a dream. A nightmare. Anything but what it is.

'You know what my dad did? I mean, you have to. You can't not know.'

'Yes.'

'What I did for him?'

How do I answer that question? 'I know,' I say, 'I knew. Even if I couldn't put it into words. From the day you threatened fat Jenny.'

You couldn't have looked at him and not known. More than mere protectiveness. He'd been angry. He'd been...exactly who he's always been.

'Why would they want to kill you?' I ask. 'You're family.'

Family. As in the Addams. The Mansons. He coughs, but it's a minor thing. An irritant in his throat. When he turns back to look at me, I try to read into those eyes some semblance of an emotion I might understand

But I get nothing. It's like looking into a mirror that reflects only shadows, black on black.

'They thought I...betrayed them. What Dad...told me.'

'Did you?'

'No.'

'Did they –?'

He coughs again. This time, it's no irritant. He's actually trying to laugh. Like his speech, it's a damaged and broken noise, something not quite real about it; a poor imitation of human sound.

'Did they ask me?' he says, and this time the laugh doesn't stop him from talking. It comes out like an exclamation mark, a final flourish on the end of a sentence. 'You never understood...never.., Your mother...protected you.'

'If she was still alive...'

He shakes his head. 'A Scobie never...strays far. What Dad... told me when I tried to...when I was young. You're...a Scobie.... Like me.'

It's true.

Glasgow born and bred, every one of us. We never leave the city. Not for long, anyway. Something always pulls us back. More than just the city. Like cats with an instinct for home, we just wind up working our way back to where we started from.

'It's all…bullshit,' he says. 'All…of it. Family. Loyalty…'

He looks for a moment like he wants to say something else. His lips move, and maybe he's forming a word, but then he turns away again.

'I'm sorry it had to be you.' he says.

'Just let me go,' I say. 'I won't –' The sentence dies on my lips when he brings up the gun and presses it against the side of my head. The metal is warm and presses against my skin.

'I will kill you,' he says. 'I will…kill you. If you don't…do as I say.' I believe him then, as much as I believed when he said he was sorry.

I don't turn my head, but swivel my eyes so I can see him. Suddenly, he's no longer Cousin Ray, but he's the monster and the killer I always knew he was. My earlier instincts about the truth of who he is beneath the skin are confirmed. There is no doubt in my mind. He doesn't want to kill me, but if I get in his way, he won't hesitate.

He lets his gun arm drop. Slow. Eyes on me the whole time, sizing me up, working out whether I believe him.

I do.

'What do you want?' I ask.

He doesn't answer. Instead, he barks out another cough. This one more violent. A clenched fist stifles it. When he's done, I grab at the hand, pull him towards me. He turns with the motion. I want him to look at me, to not ignore the question.

There's blood on his hands.

'Ray?'

He smiles. Guilty. Pretend-playful. Keeping a naughty secret, but not one that really matters.

Except it does.

That cough... That hacking noise that keeps erupting from his lungs.

He's been coughing up blood.

John

'Where in the name of Christ's holy bicycle have you been?'

Burke on the other end of the line, blasting me. Barely listening to what I have to say. He's been waiting for this moment. Finally, he's in the right.

Remember the way he looked at me when I first came into his office:

Like he was thinking, *Prick*. At the time, he was probably right too.

Going undercover, you really do need a degree of self-doubt. Can't be too comfortable in your own skin. Why? You need to slip inside someone else's. And make everyone else believe it.

If I didn't have my own doubt in spades, Burke had always happy to provide it.

I believed in the force. Wanted to do my part. But truth was I didn't want to be a copper. Being in uniform, being part of one big machine, that part didn't appeal. Maybe because I'd watched too many Westerns on the telly when I was a lad. Wanted to be the lone hero, the sheriff come into town to clean things up his own way. Undercover, you could be part of the solution but you didn't have to obey the same rules everyone else did.

Idealism? Aye, well maybe it was. You don't just get cynical overnight.

Crawford, the SIO on the operation, had seen what I was about, thought it would be an asset, while Burke yelled loud about my commitment to the cause, but not the job, being a liability.

And now he got to play the smartarse saying, *Told you so.*

'We were going to pull you out, you utter shiting cockmonkey! Things were too hot, and then you just…you just vanish!'

I'm several streets away from the Crow now. Getting the fuck out before the police arrive. Could hear the sound of sirens even before I reached the end of the road. Shots fired? On the street?

Someone's calling that in.

I'm thinking maybe re-establishing contact wasn't the right move after all.

'I –'

'Something else is going on, right? That's why you went back? Starting to get a little too used to their company? That it? You need a good bloody shrink, you wanky wee tosspot!'

Talk about my issues with professionalism? Pretty sure most of those names were on the forbidden list when it came to talking to subordinates.

Burke's the kind of boss lets off steam whether you're comfortable or not. Can only imagine how he is in briefings. Probably lets Crawford do all the talking, holds his tongue until they're done.

I'm out on the street while he yells down the line at me. Pacing the pavement, shoulders hunched, voice *sotto*. Looking around, in case I recognise anyone. Sooner or later someone's going to wonder where I am.

The Scobies and their assembled associates will be closing ranks.

Like the old man said, I'm one of them now. They'll want me close.

And this tube on the other end of the line wants me to run to Mummy? Throw myself into the welcoming embrace of the constabulary, forget all the work I've put in over the last few years? Admit defeat?

I say, calmly as I can, 'This is the perfect opportunity. They're going to implode without the old man. Let me stick around, get the shite on everyone. I can – '

'Get your head around the fact that this operation is over. I don't care who the shooter was. It's pretty bloody clear that they're whoever took out Raymond. And now they're out to finish the job. Putting you in the firing line.'

Word hasn't filtered back, then. About Raymond's miraculous return from the dead. Aye, there's the rub. Burke and Crawford still have no idea about the switch I made at the hospital. The

80

young doc's probably still playing secret agent, thinking he's doing his civic duty by pretending that my star witness died overnight, thinking he was James Bond, switching corpses with some poor John Doe to protect the man's identity.

Oh, to be that young and stupid.

Instead of this old and stupid.

'This operation should have been over weeks back. You thrust your cock in too deep, and now you can't pull out...' He took a deep breath. Making a pantomime of the moment so I'd understand. When he spoke again, his voice was at a lower register, a soothing tone, the kind you use when you want someone to think you've just apologised. 'Listen, I've seen this before. Not the first time anyone's lost it on an undercover. Especially deep as you are. You have to know that what I'm saying's the right thing to do...'

I can practically hear the switch going off in his head. He's lost me with the angry shtick, so he's changed tacks for the old sympathetic, *we're all in this together* shite.

Sod it.

I say, 'Can't talk,' hang up. Not without some small satisfaction.

I can't pull cover. Not yet.

This is both sides against the middle I need Burke to believe that all I'm thinking about taking down the Scobie family, that in the end, all I care about is making the biggest bastard bust that the Scottish force has ever known.

This operation was supposed to provide proof for the new Scottish Government that working together is the best thing for all modern branches of law enforcement. That great things can happen when resources are pooled. When the SCDEA is gone, along with Lothian and Borders, our originally joined-up effort will fall under the purview of the newly formed Scottish police force. A victory here will show the value of co-operation.

Aye, we're all in it together.

Better together, I'd guess you'd say.

I have to make my decision.

Turn myself in and let the Scobie family go to hell?

Sure, if Ray's out for revenge, blood will run in the city streets before the evening's out. Maybe it won't end in a court case, but it will mark the end of the Scobie family, no question. They'll be scattered, fragmented and screwed.

Someone will come in and pick up the pieces. Probably Buchan. But that won't be my problem. I'll be too busy cooling my heels in cell built for one when they realise just how far off the reservation I've gone.

I switch SIMs once more. Dial a number I know without looking will have been trying to call me.

Anthony says, 'Where the fuck're you?' with no preamble.

Listen to his tone, you have to wonder what separates him from Burke. The thin blue line? Has it ever really meant anything?

'Could ask you the same question.'

'He who fights and runs away...'

...is a bloody coward.

'Right,' I say, non-committal.

'Saying something?'

'Nothing.'

'Good answer, ya prick. You were there, saw what happened?'

'He killed your dad. And then he killed Neil. He wants you next.'

'And Kat?'

I don't answer right away. Make like I'm thinking it over. 'She's alive. I know it. She's his insurance. Wrong place at the wrong time. You know how your brother works, Tony. Doesn't kill anyone unless he has to. Isn't that what he always says? Unless they're a target or they're in his way or they're a threat. Kat never did anything to him.'

'He's a fucking psycho, my brother.'

Pot, meet kettle.

'No,' I say. 'He's something else. A psycho...doesn't kill indiscriminately...'

82

Who's talking, now? John the cop? John the crooked accounts assistant? John the guy who's in love with the gentle redhead?

If I look in a mirror, who's going to look back at me?

'Whatever, man. Hate to be the one to break it to you, but my cousin's dead. Same as Neil. Same as Dad.' He sniffs twice. Not with sadness or tears. And I get it, why he doesn't sound like he's in mourning Little arse bollock's high, off his nut with whatever powder he could get his grubby little hands on.

I say, 'We need to call the cops. This is this is beyond…'

'What the shit, man? You off your tits?'

'Think you can sweep this under the carpet?'

'Think I'd even waste breath on those bawbags?'

I can hear the pride in his voice. He thinks he's upholding a proud Scobie tradition. In his mind, it's us and them: the family and the enemy.

Except his dad used to talk to the cops all the time. Long time ago, when the police tried to work with men like Derek Scobie in an attempt to douse the violence on Scotland's streets. It had been a short-lived truce, but it had happened, proving once and for all that men like Derek Scobie work from a vested self-interest rather than any political or ideological standpoint.

It was pragmatism of a sort.

And it had skipped the new generation of criminal. Passing by men like Anthony, who grew up under the auspices of a society fostered by the Thatcher slogan: *Greed is good*. Looking out for themselves, and every other bugger could go piss up a tree.

Anthony Scobie would rather die than work with the cops. Not because of some grand statement, but because he was so damn self-centred that he couldn't do anything to go against his own self-image.

'I'm calling the police,' I say. 'Kat's still alive, and –'

'And fuck you,' Anthony says. 'You pathetic pishbag. Think you're safe? He said he was after me, Fat Dunc, all the ones that killed him. Think he doesn't know you were there? How you voted

83

that night? Think you're safe? You're not a citizen any more, you wee nyaf. You're as deep in the shite as the rest of us.'

I hesitate.

'What you're going to do, pal, is you're going to help me find my prick of a brother. Finish what we started. Then we're going to do all the crap my dad never had the stomach for. We're going make sure everyone knows the name Scobie. And that it makes them shite their breeks.'

He hangs up.

I look at the phone in my hand and then put it away. Look around, wonder if anyone's noticed me, the way I am, thinks maybe I'm some sketchy wee prick dealing drugs in the middle of suburbia.

But no-one seems to notice. Or care.

I figure on grabbing a number 4 bus out to Newton Mearns, but I'm a few minutes from the nearest stop. The walk might do me good, of course. But there's a taxi with its light on heading my way, so I hail him, climb in the back.

'Where to, bud?' the driver's voice coming metallic across the intercom.

I give the address, sit back. Consider hitting the button so that he can't hear me and gets the idea I don't want to chat. Not that it really makes too much of a difference. Cabbies come in two particular breeds – those that want to talk and those that are in it for the quiet drive. Lucky for me, mine is the second breed. Gives me a chance to think.

The original plan is now FUBAR.

What I'd been thinking: get Burke and Crawford someone willing to testify, then sod off sharpish.

The whole thing had been planned. The tickets were ready. Two days' time, one seat booked. Business class, of course. Paid on one of the cloned cards Anthony sometimes dealt in. I'd got the tickets right after figuring Ray was for turning. The idea had been to get the hell out, while the rest of the Scobie family implode, and the cops swoop in like vultures.

I'd been thinking about changing my mind, maybe doing the right thing. Why I'd shown my face at the wake: trying to find another way to give Crawford and Burke what they wanted. Show them I wasn't such a bad guy after all. Either way, the plan was to find a mark, get them to hand themselves in and then get lost, sharpish.

Start again. Like a computer game: hit reset, get another chance at life.

But things have changed.

Whether it's working with the cops or working with Anthony Scobie, I have to do something. I have to try and save Kat. Not just because I still love her, if I ever really did. But because she shouldn't be involved in any of this. It's my fault she's in this situation. I can't just leave it at that.

There are things I'm done that I'm not proud of, but I can live with them. But this... We all have lines. This, I realise, might just be mine.

Maybe I'm not such a complete bastard after all.

Kat

What my mother hated most was the blood. Coughing up little pieces of herself. Everything that was her falling away, one dark glob at a time.

It made me sad. It made her angry. But that anger was tempered by exhaustion. The kind that started inside, like the rot. Became all-consuming. She loathed that too. Told me in a moment of weakness that even waking up exhausted her, made her feel like no matter what she did, she was losing battle.

The blood was a physical reminder of the thing inside her. Something she couldn't deny or blame on something else. The sight of blood couldn't be shrugged off or denied.

The slow, creeping, unstoppable death took residence inside her. Coughed her up piece by piece.

Cancer.

The ugliest word I've ever known. The closest I've ever got to death. The closest I've ever wanted to be.

• • •

'It's nothing,' Ray says. 'Look at…me. Fuck's sakes… Look…at me.'

Slowly, I turn around and look at his melted skin, thinned-out hair, ill-fitting clothes. The blood flecking the corners of his mouth. He is a real-life monster, a nightmare given physical presence.

I think I smell something. Roasted pork, perhaps. It's faint, tickling the back of my nostrils. I don't feel hungry. I feel nauseous. Dizzy.

I should be terrified. I should scream.

Look at him, a voice in my head says. *Remember what he's done. Be afraid.*

This is Ray. The man who saved me from the playground bullies. My avenging angel.

He killed a boy who hurt you. You never wanted that.

Was that the only way he knew how to deal with problems? Death. Violence. Was he born a monster? Or made that way by his father, his brother, the world he came into?

Did he save me because it was the right thing to do?

Or because of what his dad had drummed into him about family?

I say, 'Do you remember…what you did for me? When I was seventeen…when…'

'The…lad who cheated…on you?'

'Yes.'

He nods. 'Do you…know what…I did?' It doesn't seem strange

to him that I'm asking about something that happened almost ten years ago.

'Was he the first man you killed?'

'No.' How do I respond to that?

'How many?'

He shakes his head. Either he doesn't know or he doesn't want to say.

'He was...he was the first...I chose.' He doesn't seem to know how to form the thought, how to tell me what he's thinking. Then: 'Did anyone ever tell you about my condition?'

'That there was something wrong with you?'

'Yes,' he says. 'Something...wrong.' His features twist uncomfortably, lips move up on side, that plastic skin wrinkling. Smiling?

'Beyond killing people?' I try not to laugh as I speak, but it's hard. There's a surrealism to our conversation that makes me wonder if this whole day – maybe my whole life – hasn't been a dream.

'Aye. Beyond that.' He hesitates.

I wonder if he's ever had this long a conversation with anyone before. He was always a man of few words; the strong silent type taken to the extremes of machismo. Preferring to communicate with a look or a gesture.

Or worse, as I was beginning to realise.

'So tell me,' I say. Remembering when we were younger, how I'd treat it like a game, trying to talk to him. But this Raymond is even more closed off than the one I remember.

He takes a deep breath. Coughs gently. No blood this time. Just killing time.

'When I...was a wee man...I bit things. Nothing unusual. Lots of children do it. But I bit...myself. Hands. Fingers. Would bleed. But...wouldn't stop. Frightened Mum...and Dad,'

He smiled, or at least his warped face crinkled into the approximation of one. If you didn't listen to what he was actually saying you could imagine he was reminiscing about the happiest

87

moments of his childhood: fairgrounds, candy floss, getting to ride on the big wheel where he could see across the rooftops of the city and so far beyond to the horizon, where possibilities seemed infinite and enticing to a young child.

But he was talking about biting and blood and the fact that he didn't know what was happening.

And didn't care.

'It continued. Didn't grow out of it. Was tested. All the time. Tests every day. I'd fall over...and not cry. Trapped my...hand in...a drawer. Broke fingers. Couldn't...didn't understand...why they stopped...working. Doctors said...I was slow. Mental retardation. That was the...phrase.'

Aye, it was. Back in the day. The 1980s: ignorance's last gasp. At least in the mainstream. 'But that wasn't what was wrong?' The Ray I knew was sharp, intelligent. Cunning in his own way. He just didn't like to talk was all.

'Later...they...found the truth. Congenital...insensitivity...to pain.' He takes a deep breath, starts coughing again, with that turn of the head so he doesn't have to face me. The arm comes up to cover his mouth. I think about the blood spitting from between his lips, spattering the material of his jacket. He recovers, turns back to face me.

I think about that for a second. Can't imagine it.

'Understand pain. Feel pressure. Degrees. Know when I'm touching something. But pain...doesn't register. Don't know when...something's hurting me...when there's...too much pressure. When something's broken or...' he trails off. I wonder how long it's been since he's talked about this with anyone outside of a doctor. Or if he's even talked to a medical professional since childhood. Surely if it was as bad as he's telling me, he'd have been in hospitals most of his childhood. So why don't I know about it? Of course, he's ten years older than me. I missed a lot of his life. And our family are good at keeping secrets. Never trust an outsider.

Ray tells me how Uncle Derek had been prepared for the worst.

A child who doesn't feel pain isn't Superman. He's more vulnerable than any kid who screams his head off the moment he gets a scratch or a bump.

I understand. I trained to be a nurse. Know what pain is, why we need it. I've never come across Ray's condition, but then if it's as rare as he claims, there's no reason I would have.

Pain is the body's way of alerting us to a problem. Without pain it's tough to tell when something's wrong, when you need to get yourself checked out. Ray tells me about severe cases of the condition, where people have died from infections because they had no idea that a piece of grit or duct was stuck in their eyes. Or others who scratched themselves on nails or branches, never noticed, never did anything and then wound up losing their limbs.

Or worse.

'I'm lucky,' he says, '...not so bad. Can still sweat.' There were cases, he tells me, of people so immune to pain, whose nerve receptors were so shut off, that they couldn't sweat or even tell when it was time to go the bathroom. Without sweat, your body suffers. If you don't go to the bathroom, your body suffers. Basic facts of medical science that anyone with rudimentary training could understand.

I remember a few years back, some student coming in with kidney stones that got trapped in his urethra. He was in agony, the trapped stone had caused a backlog – over a pint of urine waiting to escape, the lad unable to deal with the pain which some schmuck GP had thought was appendicitis. Had some enterprising senior nurse not thought to do an ultrasound on him, he'd have been dead.

'Some...poor bastards,' Ray says, 'Carry an alarm...tell them... when to go...to the toilet. Otherwise...they'd forget.'

So Ray's lucky. Take your luck where you can.

Variants of his condition, he tells me, can come with other problems. Mental health issues are not uncommon.

'Like depression?'

He shakes his head. 'And...others,' he says.

The car begins to feel like a confessional. I always hated confessionals.

We're closed in, locked together in darkness. He's telling me things that I'm sure he hasn't talked to anyone about in a very long time.

Why me? Because I'm here? Because I'm his cousin?

Because no-one else has asked him?

He reaches out with the hand he hasn't coughed into. I try not to flinch, but I still struggle with the fight or flight instinct. His heavy fingers grab my hair. Not roughly. More like taking hold of a delicate silk curtain, admiring the way it feels against his skin. I let him rub my hair between his fingers. Nothing threatening or sexual. More a longing for something he knows he can never have.

How can you trust a man you watched kill his own father? A man you know whose response to a threat is to remove it in the most permanent fashion possible?

Is it the same way that people make friends with lions? A leap of faith? Trusting that the odds are in your favour?

I don't want to end up like Uncle Derek.

Or Neil.

I watched him die in front of me. Saw the red blossom in his chest, his body give in and fall to the ground. I watched the life leave his body. Nothing spiritual about the experience. No great mysteries revealed, just the ugliness and indignity of death.

Now I was calm, I had the space to think about what had happened, realise how inhuman and distanced my reaction had been at the time. Realise that,

I let him die.

Didn't do or say anything. And the truth is that I thought, as he fell to the ground, *this is no less than he deserves.* Does that make me a bad person?

Neil had been an aging lech. Wasn't blood, wasn't family. I tolerated him because he was a friend of Uncle Derek's. And in the end, watching him die, I hadn't felt anything beyond a sense that one way or another, he'd always been going to die like that.

Does my own darkness manifest itself differently?

I have never gone to the police. Always refused to assist them in their enquiries. Never dobbed on a family member, reproached them for what they've done. I've simply refused to join in. Steadfastly created a life that allows me a level of deniability. And then, even when it got too much, what I did was leave. I didn't say anything to the police, didn't break the code of silence. Simply walked away, tried to pretend I was better than them.

And I am. I am.

Ray is still touching my hair. Suddenly he grabs a fistful and pulls me over to him. The smell of rotting flesh gets worse. My stomach turns. The insides of my nasal cavities stings.

He forces me to look at him.

'Don't...' he says, 'think this...changes anything.' He takes a deep breath. 'I will...kill you. If... I have to.'

'I believe you.'

Ray looks like a monster.

But then, we're all monsters. All of us Scobies. On the inside. Ray's skin has been burned away. He can't hide the truth from himself, or anyone else, any more.

Part of me thinks that maybe Ray has the right idea.

That we, the Scobies, all of us, might deserve to die.

John

Tony's house in Newton Mearns. A new-build bungalow he thinks is smart, the kind of home to aspire to. Small lawn out front, back garden paved over. Everything about the place is boxy and impermanent. His dad's palace out in Newlands has character. This place cost a bomb and has no soul.

The taxi pulls over and I pass the driver too much cash, let him keep the difference. I climb out, pull my jacket tighter. The city clouded over about an hour ago, and now there's a fine mist in the air that soaks coolly through my clothes.

I walk to the front, knock three times and walk in.

Anthony's in the front room with Wayne and Pete. All three look up. Serious expressions.

All the money he has, his furniture still looks like a cheap job lot. Nothing in the room speaks of taste or even comfort. Like he saw what was advertised the most on TV, went in and asked for that.

'Where's Dunc?'

'To bollocks with the fat bastard,' Anthony says. 'He's gone to ground. Into a hole, pissing himself with fear. Same as you were going to do.' He laughs. Gestures expansively in my direction. 'This daft wee prick was going to call the cops.'

I wonder if anyone's going to jump me.

Pete shakes his head. 'No need for them, pal.'

Wayne says, 'We got the connections. And the tools.'

As well as dealing in the hard stuff, the lads supply hardware to anyone with enough scratch. Handguns. Rifles. A limited line in explosives. They've both done time, but rather than learning valuable lessons about contributing, they treated incarceration like a criminal convention; built their list of contacts, expanded their reach. Whisper was that most of their weapons came from former IRA dealers looking for new opportunities in a post-armistice world.

I say, 'Your plan is...is to kill him?'

Anthony says, 'Aye. Before he kills me. It's a brother eat brother world. Keep up, pal.'

'You... we already fucked up killing him,' I say. 'And that was when we had a plan. Time to prepare.'

Pete says, 'Thanks to you, we know the car he's driving.'

Wayne nods. 'It's a start. Better than nothing.'

Anthony says, 'And I know my brother's old contacts. He's not working alone. He's got the guns from somewhere. Someone's been holing him up, too. I find out who that is, I'll fuck them up. And then...' He pauses, relishing the moment, as though he's been waiting for it all his life, 'I'll kill my brother.'

Kat

Nineteen years old.

A gentle patter against my bedroom window.

That's what I remember.

Like those American movies where the girl is woken from sleep. And she gets up – hair always perfect, of course – and goes to see what the noise is. Discovers her boyfriend trying to wake her without disturbing the parental units.

Of course, there was no handsome quarterback boyfriend with a gentle heart waiting for me in the back garden. Not even John Cusack with a boom box. Not how things happen in the Southside. Instead, it was my cousin Anthony, half hidden in shadow, trying not to set off the rear garden lights Dad had installed a couple of years previously.

Motion-activated rear garden lights. Talk about your status symbols.

'What're you doing?'

'The fuck does it look like?'

In the still of early morning, even a harsh whisper sounded like Brian Blessed roaring at the top of his lungs

I hesitated. Considered slamming the window, getting some ear plugs and letting Tony freeze his arse out there in the pre-dawn cold.

Then he stepped out where I could see him. Covered in blood. Enough that you knew he'd been in a good scrap. One where the other guy came off worse.

My first coherent thought: he shouldn't have been wearing a white shirt.

'Let me in.'

Okay, maybe not some teen romance. More a vampire film. One where the idiot, virginal girl lets the bloodsucking fiend into the house. And once he's inside, that's it, game over.

I let him in the kitchen door, sneaked him up to my room. Telling myself, what's the harm? He's family after all. On the upstairs landing, the floorboards creaked. We stopped stock-still, like kids in the playground playing at Sleeping Lions.

I expected Mum to come out, see Tony, snap completely. But nothing happened.

We stood like that maybe thirty seconds before Tony started moving again. I was another ten seconds behind him.

When I closed the door to my room, he undressed in front of me like it was the most casual thing in the world. Stripped down to his boxers. Gave me this odd little look, cocking his head to one side before grabbing the spare dressing gown, the light brown one I'd worn until I was sixteen and never quite found the time to throw out. It was frayed around the edges, and didn't quite fit him properly. All the same, it was better than a blood-spattered shirt. He didn't look so scary any more. Just a little ridiculous.

Which meant I could breathe normally.

I said, 'What happened?'

He didn't reply. Went to the window and looked outside. I'm not sure what he expected to see. The view wasn't great. The most you could really see was next door's garden that backed onto ours. And, occasionally, the sight of the neighbours making love in the upper-rear bedroom. When friends slept over, we'd watch and giggle as their loose flesh jiggled around. Maybe they thought they looked hot, but mostly they just looked like a pair of drowning walruses. But Tony wasn't looking to perv, he was looking out there like he could see the whole city laid before him. Trying to see what it was he had been running from.

I said it again: 'What happened?'

'Nothing. Some prick picked a fight. I finished it.' More than a dash of pride in his explanation.

Tony, twenty-one, already on a steady diet of powder and booze. Snorted rather than injected on some messed up principle he had about HIV. Although I knew for a fact that he didn't use condoms, good Catholic boy that he was. Not through personal experience, of course, but reliable anecdotal evidence. He was, as with all my family, a mass of contradictions. None of them good.

'I'm drinking,' he said, finally turning away from the window, sitting on the far end of my bed. I was glad of the distance between us, sitting cross-legged on one of the large pillows near the head. Aye, we're family, but I'm aware that when he gets high, he forgets the most basic social conventions, never mind the absolutes. He'd never tried anything before, but a little warning voice at the back of my brain slickly and sickly insisted there's a first time for everything.

'I'm drinking,' he said again. 'I'm drinking and this arsehole is sitting next to me at the bar. Pissed, of course. Weedy wee bollocks. Thick glasses. Michael Caine, aye? So, anyway, he's sitting next to me, trying to chat up the wee girl behind the bar. She's fit, like. I mean, serious set of legs, nice tits, great arse. Big glasses, like, but you can't have everything.' He grinned. 'And so the tube is trying to pick her up and failing. What I do is tip her the wink. And she's on me. I mean, really. Maybe it's so's the eejit gets the hint, or maybe she knows a good thing when she sees it. But still he keeps trying. Doesn't get the message. I decide he's just drunk and because I'm a magnanimous prick, let it go. Long as he isn't trying to cop a feel, I figure she can just bat it off. Job like that, guess you get used to it.'

Who said chivalry was dead?

'So I get up to go take a piss and he follows me. Into the bathroom. Believe it? Not like we're piss pals or something. He's following me because he wants to tell me to lay off and you know he's onto a good thing with the bird, and he wants me to leave her the fuck alone. So I tell him he's being a prick and reckon that's it, but he doesn't let up.'

'So you hurt him?'

'What, you think I'm just a thug? I'm a Scobie. You know how Dad tells it, we bend the rules, but we're good, honest people. What you see, it's what you get. Aye? Besides, he starts it. The prick, I mean. Swings the first punch. I just fight back.'

Maybe with anyone else you could believe it was just a fight that got out of hand. But then you look at Tony and what you see in his eyes is a powder-fuelled lust.

He gets off on fighting the same way other men get off on women. In fact, I think he might be more into the fighting. Because that adrenaline high was still in him. He was shaking at the memory. Not with fear. Excitement. He was turned on, I'm sure of it.

He told me in detail about how the fight went down. The other guy swinging the first punch. Tony stepping aside, grabbing the guy's arm, twisting it, pulling and smacking the guy's face off the bathroom wall. Should have been enough to end any decent fight, but of course this was Anthony Scobie and he couldn't just let it go. He followed through, fast, when the other guy went down. Smashed the poor idiot's face against the sink, smacking bone against porcelain until the white stained through red. The other man's body had finally gone limp. But even then it wasn't enough for my dear, dear cousin.

When he told me what he had done, his eyes lit up like a child remembering their favourite birthday cake. Reliving the experience as he told me about. Didn't matter to him whether I was paying attention or not, he just wanted to talk, tell someone about what he had done.

My cousin. The psychopath.

What I should have done was throw him out, or turn him into

the cops. But I let him stay the night. He took the floor, of course, and I slept with the covers pulled tight around me, like a cocoon.

In the morning, when Mum found Tony in the kitchen running his clothes through the washing machine and wearing my old dressing gown, looking oh-so-manly, we told her that he'd turned up drunk and I'd let him sleep it off on the couch. He'd been sick on his clothes, which was why he has to use the washing machine.

Mum knew what was going on, of course. But we were all complicit in my cousin's psychopathy. She'd never turn him in. Neither would I. And I think that was the day she realised what she'd done, drumming into me the codes that she wanted me to reject. It was too late for me, same as it had once been too late for her.

I was a Scobie.

There would never be any doubt.

Screwed up. Like all the rest of them.

• • •

I need to clear my head.

Stop thinking about the past. Get a better look at Ray's injury. Do what he asks. Make sure he's fit for purpose. If you do it, he'll let you live. If you cross him, he'll kill you.

Some choice.

By now, Anthony would be looking for Ray. Have people out on the streets. He knew the car we were driving. His ear would be pressed to the ground.

Uncle Derek had more than a handful of police in his pocket. Would they know what had happened by now? Would they be dancing on the old man's grave? Looking for revenge?

I don't know what to do.

So I tell Ray that I need to look at his wounds.

He says, 'I know…I'm dying.'

'Want to be dead before your brother?'

He shakes his head.

'Then trust me.'

He doesn't need to say what he's thinking. I've already got the message.

I take a deep breath, try not to think about the past or even the events of earlier this evening. I try to focus on one thing: finding a way to help Ray, to stop the bleeding.

I exhale. Close my eyes for a moment. Open them again.

Start the engine.

John

Pete and Wayne are gone. Hitting the streets. Beating the bushes. Doing what they need to do. Now it's just me and Tony.

I tried to persuade him that I needed to be out there doing something too. But he tells me that I'm the only family he has left now.

He still thinks Kat is dead. Or good as.

Maybe he's right. Makes it worse, him asking me to stay.

Besides, as he reminds me, I'm still just a citizen. I don't know his world. Not really. Helping plant a bomb doesn't make me capable of doing what men like Pete and Wayne do.

We're in the front room. I'm watching him do lines, near constant. It's a nervous tick. Like picking at fingernails or scratching balls. I say, 'What do we do when he's dead?'

Tony looks up, wipes the back of his hand across his nose. 'Show people that there's a new king in town. No-one messes with me.'

'Aye?'

'Aye, not even my brother. Don't be naïve, John. Too late for the little boy lost crap. You know what's at stake. You're a killer now.'

'No,' I say. 'A minute ago I was a citizen.'

'You're a killer by intent. You thought all we were going to do with that bomb was scare my brother?'

I don't answer.

How did I get here? Who am I? Really, who am I? A cop or his cover? Or something else entirely?

I think about the man I saw in the mirror a few days ago, the one who berated me for everything that I'd done. I haven't seen him since. Perhaps he realised the situation was hopeless. Perhaps he was the last vestiges of my conscience.

Perhaps he's just ashamed.

I had no choice. I did everything I could to try and make sure that the bomb never went off, I'm sure of it. But Tony was there the whole time. Encouraging me. Telling me how if I didn't do it, I'd be as dead as Ray. 'You wanted to be a gangster, get a piece of this life, you've got it, pal.'

When it was done, after we fled the scene, he took me to bar, bought me a drink. Place was a dive, iron bars on the windows, scuffed floor, lighting so low most of the drinkers had the skin tone of corpses. We sat at a corner table, and I could smell the vomit on trousers, and he said, 'Today, my son, you are a man.'

That was when he spread out three lines, told me to go wild. I looked around, my heart doing the Riverdance. No-one even looked at us. No-one in the place gave a monkeys what a man like Anthony Scobie did, long as he left them alone. So I snorted back the drugs, convinced myself that this was all in the name of my cover.

Not allowing myself to believe I was beginning to like it.

'I know what I did,' I tell him, shaking off memories, trying not to think about the part I played in the attempt on Ray's life. I look at the pictures over his fake fireplace, the family portraits that try to lie to the casual observer.

'Then you know what you are.'

'Sure.'

He takes a package out from his jacket pocket. Spreads out six lines, separates them with his credit card. Waves at me to come over, sit beside him. 'Take the edge off.'

'No.'

'No?'

'I need the edge.'

He laughs, throws back his head. Brays it out like those kids in the *Pinocchio* film before they turn into donkeys. The phone rings.

'Get that.'

I hesitate a moment too long.

'Get it!'

I answer neutral. On the other end of the line, Fat Dunc says, 'Put Anthony on.'

I hand over the phone, tell Tony who it is. He shakes his head.

I say to Fat Dunc, 'He's busy.'

'Getting high? Always his answer. When there's trouble.'

I look at Tony. Sitting back on the sofa now, arms wide across the back, legs splayed. Content, the high is kicking him hard. I walk away, turn my back on the psycho prick.

'You're okay?' I ask down the line.

'Why wouldn't I be?'

'What happened today?'

'The police were here.'

'Oh.'

'I need to talk to him. Tell him to call me when his fucking brain's working again.'

'Sure.'

'Not on this line.' He rattles off a mobile number. I commit it to memory. Hang up. When I tell Tony, he says, 'Old prick probably told the polis everything. Frail old fuck. Used to be he was somebody. Back in the day.'

'I know.' I read Dunc's files. Committed them to memory. Back in the '70s and '80s, he'd been a real figure of fear. The kind of enforcer you'd have paid good money to keep on side. But for whatever reason, he'd been loyal to Derek Scobie for reasons that had nothing to do with cash. Did friendship really mean something to these people?

'Now he's just a scared old man. His time has been and gone, man.'

I remember how Dunc was at the funeral. Looking back, you had to wonder if he knew something was going down. Kat had told me he'd been strongly hinting that she needed to leave just about five minutes before Ray showed up.

Tony said it himself, Ray had to have some help from the inside, someone who was protecting him, who had helped him to stay alive this long, got him the guns he needed, the car.

I don't say anything to Tony. Figure I'm getting paranoid. Contact high, just being in the same room with someone as off their face as Tony.

Or else all those drugs I took in the name of my cover never really left the system.

I say, 'Maybe you should call him. Maybe he knows something. Maybe he –'

'Maybe he nothing!' Tony's on his feet. Kicks the glass coffee table over, strides to where I am and thrusts his face into mine. I blink as warm spit hits my face. His breath has a sour smell.

At the back of my brain, primeval instincts urge me to get away. But I remain where I am. Takes all my willpower too.

'I think you're forgetting who you are, pal. Telling me what to do, who to talk to. I'll deal with this the way I see fit. I'm the king shit now. When I kill my brother, I'm going to mail his bastard head to the police, let them know what happens to anyone gets in my way. And his balls, I'm going to send them to that arsewipe, Buchan. So he knows that it's his getting cut off next.'

Tony's eyes lock on mine. They're empty. No humanity. Just a lust for violence. A contempt for everything he ever looks at. I've pushed this too far. He's finally going to kill me. And maybe that's for the best.

But what he does is turn away. Walk across the other side of the room. Keeping his back to me. Breathing slow and steady. His back rises and falls. He's hunched over. Animal-like.

Someone knocks at the door.

Loud. Insistent. A special kind of knock. The kind of knock that gets attention. A copper's knock. Kind of knock you learn day one out on the beat and keep the rest of your career.

I clear my throat. 'I'll get it,' I say.

Tony doesn't say anything.

I walk to the front door. Take two deep breaths before reaching out and opening the door.

'Was wondering if I could speak to Anthony Scobie.'

I don't say anything. Just stare at Crawford.

Wonder what the hell he's doing here.

And whether Tony really will make good on his threat.

Kat

Last time I saw Lesley Scott, she was knocking back the wine and telling Anthony what he could do with his cheap pick-up lines and even cheaper aftershave.

I never had too many close friends. Things always went wrong when they met my family. But as Lesley said, with a shrug after a few too many drinks, 'Love the person, not the family.'

First day we met at nursing school, she was the only one not to ask if I was related to 'those' Scobies.

She's got herself a new flat near the Mitchell Library. Modern interior. Private parking beneath the building. Video secure entry. The full-on cosmopolitan life. I park on the street outside, call up, tell her I just wanted to come round, say hello.

'Thought you'd left for the quiet life in the country?'

'You got any wine in?'

She laughs. Gives me the code for the underground parking. In the passenger seat, Ray remains silent. Hasn't asked what my plan is. Simply trusting me to do the right thing. I've kept my word, after all. Haven't taken him to hospital or tried to alert the police.

We take the elevator up. The interior smells new, part of the rejuvenation of the area – stylish city-centre flats for modern living. Lesley called it bachelor central when she moved in, but she likes living on her own. The flat has some nice views, and the neighbours mostly keep to themselves.

She answers the door dressed in a loose grey top and dark jeans. No shoes, just bare feet. A new haircut. Shorter than I remember, more styled. I like it. Makes her look younger. Not that she's that much older than me, maybe a few years, but you couldn't guess.

She says, 'You okay?' Stops when she sees Ray standing behind me. There's that moment where her eyes go wide, but other than that, her reaction is restrained. Given the way Ray looks, I have to admire that.

I noticed, when we left the elevator, he left a large smudge of blood where he'd been leaning against the wall.

I say, 'Sorry, can we come in?'

She tries her best not to look concerned. Fails. Waves us inside. Tries to treat Ray like she would anyone else, not staring too long at Ray's face. But she knows something's wrong. The way she lets us in quick and hurried: an ant scrambling to get its work finished before the queen gets impatient.

'I'm sorry,' I say, when she sits down on the armchair across from me and Ray. We perch on the couch. Ray's hand is inside his jacket. Reaching for that handgun, ready to move if anything goes wrong.

He doesn't want to be here. Trusted me enough to come, but doesn't know what I'm doing.

Lesley says, 'Who's this guy?'

Ray answers. I don't mind. I don't know what to say. 'Her cousin,' he says. Lets his coat drop open just enough. Lesley's face registers surprise, but she remains calm. Her eyebrows raise, but other than that and a small, startled flinch, there's no reaction.

I wonder which she sees first: the blood? Or the gun?

'Her cousin?' she says. 'I've met Kat's cousin. Tony. He was a dick. You're not Tony.'

'You're calm,' Ray says to her. 'Good. Very good. Want you to look at me.'

She is looking at him. At the gun. At the blood.

'Up here,' he says, 'Look at my face.' His voice calm. Like a therapist, or maybe a hypnotist. Despite the scratchiness, the way he talks in bursts, he manages to give the impression of a man in complete control. Derren Brown with a plastic face. 'Telling you...the truth.' He gives her a moment, and when she's looking at him, he says, 'Don't want to hurt you. Won't. Kat trusts you. She's scared... too. And she's fine. Done everything...I asked. And she's fine.'

I nod, agreeing with him. The complicity makes my stomach do flip-flops. Is this who I am? When push comes to shove, am I the person who lets the situation wash over them?

The idea makes me sick. But I still don't do anything.

'Lesley. Kat says...you're a nurse. Can help me. All I want. Help me...I'll be gone. Out of your life. Never here. Wake up tomorrow...think I was a dream. But you have to do...what I say. Think you can?'

She nods.

I watch her, try to figure what she's thinking. Hard to know, because her expression is absolutely blank. Like she's not thinking about anything at all. So completely lost in his gaze that there is no other thought for her except what he's saying, how he's looking at her.

You might think it was love, that intensity. But it's hypnotism. Ray's like the snake from the Jungle Book.

Trust in me.

'What I need... Patch me up. You work on...trauma wards. Don't need to remove...the bullet. Not an idiot. Know...it's a risk. Removing a bullet...without proper equipment. One wrong move and...That's okay. That's okay. Just need patched up. Think you can?'

Lesley finally speaks: 'You need to go to the hospital.'

'I know. I will. More important things.'

'I don't know...'

'You're not listening.' He draws attention to the gun.

'I'm listening,' she says. Then she looks at me, and I can't look back. I'm not a killer, not like my cousin, but I know that after tonight I've lost a friend.

Can you kill friendship?

No need for the Magic Eight Ball on that, when all signs point to yes. Lesley's eyes drift to the gun. Ray's holding it low and casual, like it doesn't matter.

But it does. The gun is what's keeping her quiet, making her listen. The gun, and the fact that Ray's voice is low, steady, serious.

She believes everything's he's telling her. Same as me.

John

Crawford doesn't smile. Doesn't act like he knows me at all.

Al Pacino could take lessons.

'Anthony Scobie at home?'

I graciously play the part. 'Aye, and who're you?'

Still with that poker face, he says, 'Police. I need to talk to him about his father's murder earlier today.'

'Don't know if he's in the mood for talking.'

'I'm not going to bust him.'

'You sure?'

He just grins and steps forward. Can't read his expression. I step aside, let him through. He walks down the hall like this is his own home.

'Tony, it's DCI Crawford. Remember me?'

Tony comes down the stairs. Soon as I went to the door, he was bolting it to the upstairs bathroom, no doubt trying to hide the evidence. Not that he can do much about the bloodshot eyes or the grin that's on his face like a crookedly hung picture. He looks at Crawford. 'Course I do. You're the one keeps harassing my dad.' Glances at me. 'Never getting you a job on the door, man.'

'Not his fault,' Crawford says. He looks at me. 'You don't look like the kind of company our boy here usually keeps.'

'He's my accountant,' Tony says.

Fight or flight? My sphincter tightens.

Crawford looks back at me, façade of ignorance dropping for a moment. Just his expression, not his body. I hope. Because if Tony realises something's wrong, we're all fucked.

'You have to be good with figures, working with this one,' he says. 'His family practically invented what they call creative accounting.'

'How about a wee bit of respect?'

'Because your dad's dead?'

'Think you can manage?'

'Know something? I heard a strange rumour.' Crawford moves to the sofa, sits down, giving the overturned coffee table a meaningful glance but saying nothing. 'I heard your dad was killed by your brother.'

'You're a sick bastard, you know that? My brother's dead. We… we buried him today.'

'What was left of him.'

'Get to shite.'

'Way I understood it, he was so badly burned that identification was tough.'

'It was a big explosion.'

'Still no suspects.'

'Why aren't you harassing that arsewipe, Buchan? We all know he was the one did it.'

'Tell me,' Crawford says. Like this is just a normal conversation between two old friends. 'Why are people saying Ray's the one killed your father?'

Crawford keeps looking over at me as he speaks. How much does he really know? Has the wee doctor gone and cliped on me?

106

Is Crawford here for me, not Tony?

I should walk.

But I stay.

Because it's clear from body language alone that this isn't about me. These two have history Crawford's putting on a show for Tony's benefit.

When I first started working for Crawford, I figured there was something else going on beyond the basic business of cops and robbers. Crawford's crusade against the Scobies always had an air of the personal about it. A little research gave me answers. Crawford's father was killed during what later turned out to be a gangland shooting gone wrong, back in the '80s. Possible – read definite, but not proven – connections to Derek Scobie. Maybe this was all an elaborate revenge for Crawford. Soon as the SCDEA was formed, given new powers, he applied for a transfer to the new unit, worked hard to establish a strike force dedicated to taking down the Scobies by any means possible. Made a good enough case that he got his wish.

But Derek Scobie is dead now. So it's his surviving son who's about to get it in the neck.

'You just come here to harass me?'

'No. To express my condolences. Ask if you can think of anyone who –'

'You already said it was my dead brother. Revenge from beyond the fucking grave.' Tony raises his arms and waggles his fingers like a kid playing at ghosts.

'That true?'

'Shouldn't you be sitting behind a desk somewhere?'

'Right now,' Crawford says, 'This is just gang on gang violence. Arseholes killing arseholes. I'm here to tell you, Tony, if this gets out of hand, we'll come down on you like your old man could never have dreamed. You're wearing the big boy pants now. You have a responsibility.'

'Aye?'

'Don't pretend like I'm an idiot. Don't lie to me.' He leans forward, opens the top few buttons of his shirt. 'I'm not wearing anything.' He pulls out his mobile, throws it on the table. 'No-one's listening. This is just you and me here.'

'Just you and me?'

'I came in my own car.'

Tony grins. 'Then why don't you drive back? It's bad enough without this harassment. You go catch whoever it was killed my dad. I don't know who he was. I was... I'd gone home.'

'Aye?'

'Tough day. I couldn't take the bullshit of the wake, know what I mean?'

'Guess so.'

Tony looks at me. 'Want to show the DCI here the door?'

'I can find it myself.'

'I'd rather know you were gone.' Then, to me: 'Think you can manage that?' Rebuking for letting Crawford in the door at all.

'Suit yourself.' Crawford stands. Looks me up and down as though it's the first time he's ever noticed me. 'Like this streak of piss could stop me, even if he wanted.'

I follow him out into the corridor. Crawford says, loud, 'Going to walk me to my car too.'

'If it means you'll be gone.'

We walk down the garden path, not saying a word. I stop at the gate. Crawford walks to his car. Stops with his hand on the door, looks at me.

'You need to come in, John.'

I want to look back, see if Tony's watching us out the window.

'It's going to be a bloodbath,' I say. 'Anthony's not his old man. He doesn't give two shits about the cops or anyone. The only thing that ever kept him in check was fear of his father.'

'And what about his brother? We started looking into your reports, John. Asking questions. We talked to the doctor who signed the death certificate on the poor crispy-fried John Doe got buried this afternoon. You told him to lie? Told him that the force sanctioned –'

'I… I needed time.'

'Time?'

'I was panicking, okay? I was just trying to sort everything out. Take some responsibility.'

'Good job, John. Bra-bloody-vo. That's why you need to come in. You need to come in. Look, we can work this out. Not just the deception… But…anything else you might have done too. There's nothing we can't get in front of here. If that's what's been under your collar these last few months…'

'No,' I say. 'I can keep Anthony under control. Play this out right, hand him to you on a fucking platter.'

There are things we can't get in front of.

Like my part in the attempted murder of Ray Scobie.

'You've done enough. The whole affair is screwed. We can take it from here. The Scobies are over. Your boy Ray may not have flipped on the family, but if it really was him shot his old bastard dead, he's destabilised not just the family, but the organisation.'

'He wants me here. What the fuck am I supposed to say?'

'Think of something,' Crawford says, 'Or when this is over, I can't guarantee I'll be able to protect you.'

I shrug. He opens the car door, gets inside. Drives off.

When I get back inside, Tony says, 'You two seemed pretty cosy out there.'

'He wanted me to come in, talk about what I knew.'

'What does he think you know?'

'He was on a fishing trip. That's all.'

Tony laughs. Long, loud, hard. 'Fuck me, but you're a hard man, now, eh? Little fucking number-boy's getting his first pair of balls.'

I relax a little.

Tony plants his hands on my shoulders. Firm. Like the prelude to a massage. Or a strangulation. 'Just remember, you're as fucked as anyone else. Ray gets to me, I'm telling him who planted the bomb, whose bloody fingerprints are all over that piece of shite incendiary. Don't think that just because Kat loves you and just because you used to be a citizen, it's going to stop him blowing your fucking brains out.'

I make like I understand.

Try not to think that I just made a huge mistake, giving Crawford the brush off.

Fool myself that all of this is part of the plan. That I can make everything all right again. Somehow. If I can just keep myself together.

At the back of my mind, something chuckles. And I know that I'm deluding myself, but what other choices do I have left?

Kat

Lesley bites her lip as she cleans the wound. Working slowly, taking her time.

She never took the blood or the death to heart. The reason I left the course, moved into administration, was that I always let my own empathy get in the way of treating the patient. I couldn't help but think about their pain. Lesley cared – she's always cared – but she was able to put that to one side in order to do what she had to help them. I admired that about her.

Even now, she has to be scared. But she hasn't hesitated once.

I wonder, once this is over, if she'll understand why I brought Ray here, why she was the only person I felt I could trust with this.

More importantly, will she be able to forgive me?

She takes care not to tug at the wound, to make it worse. She doesn't make an effort to actually remove the bullet. Without specialist equipment, you're just as likely to kill the patient as remove the obstruction. She cleans the wound, closing it as best she can, using plastic squares from an old bag and parcel tape to simulate a dressing. Placing the plastic over the wound and the tape around the plastic to hold it closed. One side of the square is open, allowing his skin to breath. This is detail work. Needs a steady hand and a clear mind. She goes at it slowly, conscientiously. All the time, biting gently on her lower lip. Something she always did when concentrating. Occasionally she straightens, takes a breath. Sometimes she stops for a moment, tries to convince Ray that he needs to go to the hospital.

His response is always the same: 'Just stop the bleeding.'

He's a machine. Driven. His singular purpose blinding him to anything else, including his own wellbeing.

I think about everything he's done. Everything I know. What made him this way? When did he become this thing that killed his own father, that took me hostage at gunpoint?

I'll kill you.

I can't equate that with the man I knew killed for me.

No, he didn't kill for me. That's what I failed to understand for all those years.

He killed for family. The only thing he had been raised to believe in. And now he'd been betrayed by that, and nothing mattered anymore.

I wonder if his blind focus had something to do with the fact he doesn't understand pain in the same way other people do? I want to ask him. To know the truth. There are bits and pieces of the puzzle. I know that he was home-schooled as a young child, that he was disruptive in mainstream schools. He never officially had any employment, other than the positions his father gave him in the legitimate Scobie businesses. Positions that often involved little real work. No-shows and joke jobs. Taking pity on a son who could never have a normal life? Or something else? Something darker? Creating a plausible deniability?

Raymond Scobie, who are you?

Lesley looks unsettled as she works. Concentrating. Treating this like an exam. Except there's more at stake than pass or fail.

The blood has rushed from her face. She's deathly pale. She pauses every few seconds, catching her breath, looking at him, forehead creasing. Not concern. Not in the personal sense.

He doesn't flinch or gasp or as she works the wound. Lesley's good at her job – I remember watching her at the hospital, the way she let nothing and no-one throw her off the task at hand – but she knows that something's wrong.

My cousin. The unfeeling killer. Literally.

But while he can't feel what's happening to him, the big question is: how long can he last? It's a question none of us can answer. He's still standing. That's more than most. He should have died when they burned him.

So what is keeping him alive? Hate?

Is he acting on a principle? Some code of ethics, twisted as it might seem? Is this attempt to kill his father, his brother, merely a balancing of the books? They tried to kill him, so he has to kill them. Is that how his world works?

Lesley stretches. Stands. Not easy working on her living room floor without proper equipment. She says, 'You do what you have to do. But too much exertion, you're going to… If you don't bleed out first, that bullet's going to dig in deep. Worm its way inside. Do some real damage. All I can do just now is patch you up. If I try to actually remove the bullet, you'll die. You know that. And I think you also know need to be in hospital.'

Ray nods. He stands up. It takes a bit of effort.

Lesley looks surprised. But she doesn't say anything. Maybe because she just lied to him. A hospital's no good. Not now. We both know that. The Golden Hour is long gone. Those sixty minutes where you can save a man's life have expired. All we're doing now is trying to delay the inevitable.

Ray pulls on his jeans. Moving slower, more clumsily than before. Does doesn't feel the pain, but that doesn't mean his body keeps functioning regardless. Bit by bit, he's breaking down. He has to know that.

He slips on a jumper that belonged to one of Lesley's old boy-friends. The material stretches. The blood-soaked shirt he was wearing earlier is discarded behind the sofa.

'What happens now?' Lesley asks.

Ray slips his gun into the waistband of his jeans. 'Now...go to bed. Sleep. Don't tell...anyone.'

'And if I do?'

Ray shakes his head. Walks out of the room. Moving stiff, limbs in need of oil. The Tin Man on the road to Oz squeaking, *oil can*. We hear the bathroom light click on. The sound of water running.

Lesley looks at me. 'I'm sorry,' I say.

'Your bloody family,' she says. 'Always said, soon as you could, you were shot of them. Thought you'd gone and done it too. That arsehole John maybe doing you some good, opening your eyes to the truth. Good for you, I said. And now? What's this?'

I don't have any rejoinder. When I speak, I sound almost pathetic. 'I've said a lot of things.'

Lesley says, 'I know what you're like with family, but this is bad. This is beyond... Look, we can try and do something. You distract him, I'll call the police. Bloody hell, the state he's in, we could –'

'No,' I say, 'we really couldn't.'

I think about earlier. The sound of the gunshot that killed my uncle. The expression on Neil's face as he collapsed onto his knees, then crumpled to the floor.

I take a deep breath. What comes back is a sob. I swallow, but it won't stop and I have to collapse into the closest chair. Lesley just looks at me, her expression blank. Nothing there for me to read or understand. I don't know if she's scared, angry or afraid. Maybe she doesn't even know, trying to work it out for herself.

She lets out a long breath, sits down on the couch. Her eyes are heavy. The last hour or so has taken it out of her. But she's made no move for the phone. Hasn't tried to make an escape or double-cross us. She's done her job, and now she doesn't know what to do.

'Will he hurt you?'

'I don't know.'

Not, *will he hurt me? Will he hurt you?*

I swallow back a strange, bitter anger.

'He needs me,' I say. 'If he's going to see this through. He knows that he's hurt. He can't deal with that, though.'

'I've never met anyone able to ignore pain like that. He should have been screaming the building down. Can he feel anything at all?'

'He says he's never been able to.'

Lesley nods. 'You think that's why he does what he does? Kill people, I mean?'

'How do you know that?'

'I looked in his eyes. Saw an absence. I've seen it before. The police brought in this drug dealer who killed three of his customers, ones who'd gone back on what they owed. Cut them up with a bloody samurai sword, you know, one of the ones with the curved blade? Thought he was King Cool, in the midst of a Tarantino movie. Except instead of Royale with cheese, people talked about chips and gravy. He'd been hurt, and I was the lucky one on night shift. When I was treating him, he told me his story, voice never rising, never falling. All in one flat monotone. Like your cousin there. He told me about how he killed the guys. In detail. More upset that he'd been caught so easily by the police than by what he actually did.'

'Ray had the same look?'

Ray comes back through. His face is wet, like he hasn't dried it properly. Looking closer, I see is not water, but sweat. Whether he feels it or not, he's hurting bad. Like he told me earlier, he got lucky with his condition: at least he can sweat.

I know enough to realise he might not make it through the night. Even with the bleeding temporarily abated on the outside. It's what you can't see that usually winds up killing you. Lesley's been telling him that since we arrived. And I think he knows it. But doesn't care.

'Phone?'

Lesley nods to where it sits near the window.

Ray grabs the handset, dials a number from memory.

Five seconds.

'It's me.'

He listens to whoever's on the other end of the line.

'Shut up. You know why. You fucking know. This ends tonight. Just you and me.'

He listens again. Leans against the wall, and had this blank expression like he's just waiting for the voice on the phone to just shut up. Then: 'Name the place. We end it all tonight. You. Me. The fat bastard... The traitor.' He smiles, then. 'Aye. The traitor. Undercover cop. Devious wee...prick.'

Ray hangs up. He comes over to me, puts a hand on my shoulder. The weight nearly puts me on the floor. 'You know...who he is?'

'Who?'

'The...traitor?' I shake my head. Not like I have any interest. Not my concern. One of the family wants to break ranks, it's not my business.

'Your...ex.'

'What?'

'John.'

'No.'

He nods. 'I'm sorry. Always... He...was a cop.'

'No, he was an accountant.'

'Cop. Undercover. I'm sorry.'

Does he mean it? Hard to tell. He can't look me in the eye. Never could. Ray was never a person for those intimate human moments.

But he wasn't lying. I knew that much.

•　•　•

'How come I never met your family?'

'Huh?'

He wasn't really asleep. I knew that. There was a difference when he dropped off, a change in his body, a slackening that signalled he was finally lost to the world. He would pretend, sometimes, I knew. Ignore when I touched him, tune out my voice. There were nights that he would seem tense, even after we'd made love.

'Your mum and dad. I don't even know if you have a brother or a sister. You just –'

'There's no-one.' In the dark, his voice sounded small, as though he was speaking from somewhere far away. 'Just me. No family.'

· · ·

Was that even true? I had to wonder.

Was anything John told me true? Was there a family somewhere? Not just a mum and a dad, but maybe a wife and a child.

He'd proposed to me. I'd said yes.

'How long have you known?'

'Came to…see me in hospital. Get me to…turn evidence. Against Dad. The family. His idea…revenge.'

'But you thought it would be better to kill everyone?'

'Principle.'

'That's your dad speaking. No, it's not him. I'm sorry. It's your fucking brother. The sodding psychopath!' I want to shout and scream and hit something. I want to break things. But what I do is start punching at Ray. He doesn't say anything. I might as well tickle him.

'You want to kill him too?' I ask. 'John, I mean.'

'He's not innocent. Not a…civilian. A taxpayer. He's a…copper. Soldier. Turncoat. He didn't stop…them. Didn't…do anything.' I try to say something, but all I can do is stutter nonsense. 'Betrayed you. Betrayed me. Guilty as Dad. As…Anthony. No. Worse. More.'

I shake my head. He says, 'Need…to move.' Looks at the clock on the wall. 'Not long. All over…by tomorrow.'

'What about me?' Lesley says.

Ray nods. Takes her by the arm, marches her out of the living

116

room. His gait is increasingly awkward. Hard not to notice. But he's still strong. Lesley doesn't resist. Smart girl. I follow them to the bedroom. There's a wardrobe takes up too much of the far wall. Heavy oak, double doors that pull open. A long-hosed vacuum beside it. Ray pushes her forward. 'Inside.'

She shakes her head. 'I don't like small spaces –'

'Inside.' He won't ask a third time.

Lesley understands, nods, and pulls the doors open. Steps in among the hangers and the shoes. Ray closes the door. Grabs the vacuum cleaner, uses the long nozzle as a jam through the handles and steps back. Then he nods.

'Thank you,' I say.

'For?'

'Not hurting her.'

He grunts, and we walk out, back to the living room. He unplugs the phone, stomps it underfoot. 'Clean…yourself up.'

I go to the bathroom, use Lesley's brush on my teeth. The minty toothpaste is refreshing. I rinse, and have a sudden desire for a long, cool drink of water. I pour from the tap, gulp like I've been in the desert for days. Ray, outside, says, 'Move.'

We go to the front door. He stops as we're about to leave. As though he just realised something.

'Ray?'

I see it. What Lesley saw. That blankness in his expression. The inhuman set to his face. He takes a deep breath, turns and walks back to the bedroom. I follow. Finding it hard to breathe, my chest moving in shallow gulps. I don't know what's happening, but that look in his eyes was the same one I saw when he killed his father.

He takes his gun out, turns to look at me as though daring me to make a sound.

But I can't. Even if I want to, I can't.

He's finally lost it. He told me he wouldn't hurt her. He promised, and then he kept that promise.

So what's changed? Why is he holding the gun? Lesley did

everything he asked. By the time she gets out to call the police, we'll be far away and all of this will be over.

One way or another.

So why?

He slides the nozzle from between the handles. Careful. Not making a sound. Then pulls open the door.

Lesley looks up from where she's crouched to the rear of the wardrobe. Startled. Eyes wide. Drops the mobile. The one she must have had on her the whole time.

Ray told her she couldn't call the police. Warned her what would happen.

Lesley stares at him. Tries to speak, but what she does is croak. Doesn't matter anyway. He's not ready to listen.

I say, 'No, Ray, don't –'

He raises the gun.

She says, 'Fu–'

He shoots her in the face.

She falls back.

I clap my hands to my ears, close my eyes. Like when I was a girl, scared of what might be in the dark.

The thud of her collapse is muffled. I open my eyes.

Hangers and clothes fall around Lesley. Her legs spasm out and her body jerks. Then she lies perfectly still for a moment. One final movement, and it's over. I look away, not wanting to see the blood spread out across the shoes and discarded hangers.

Ray turns to me. I try not to cry. Feel the sting in my eyes.

We leave. He holds me by the arm to force the urgency. I wish I could cry. Scream. Say something. Anything. But I let myself be led. Spent. Useless. Unable fight any of this.

All I can think about is John. What Ray told me. How my fiancé betrayed me. Betrayed my family. How none of us would be in this mess if it weren't for him.

If I ever see him again, Ray won't have to pull the trigger.

I'll do it myself.

Four

Backstabbers

2044 - 2322

John

'Come on, man,' I say. 'Don't be an eejit.'

Except for the first time in his life, he's not. First sensible thing I've ever known him to do, threaten to kill me. Tony's the one with the gun. The power.

And all I can think is,

Why didn't I see this coming?

And,

How can I put a stop to this?

Not that there are any easy answers. Had to happen, eventually. Ray's never been on my side. Never on anyone's side but his own. The phone call had one purpose only: to distract his brother from what was really going on. Knock him off balance.

Aye, that was it.

Whatever made me think I had some kind of special immunity?

'Tell me why I don't shoot you right now.'

'Because whatever Ray told you, it's nonsense. Look, he's trying to get to you. Get to us. Mess with our heads. You know it, right?'

'Aye?'

He wasn't convinced. He'd never really been a thinker. He'd always operated on his paranoid instincts.

Maybe Ray wasn't as mindless as I used to believe. I tug open my shirt, echoing Crawford earlier. 'I'm not wired.' Maybe not the best thing to do, mirror the policeman who dropped round just to mess with our heads.

'Deep undercover, you don't need to be wired. More dangerous if you are.'

'Want to take a good look at my cock? Make sure they haven't stuck something up there. Maybe it's really a microphone'

'Suck on this.' He waves the gun at me. Big barrel. Black finish. The kind of thing you could imagine Jason Statham using to fuck up some bad guys. In the movie of his life, Tony would want to be played by Statham. Even if he's got more in common with Joe Pesci.

I try to calm him down. 'Hey, man, just think about it. He wants you off balance. Ray's a smart guy. He's trying to–'

'Tell me you're not a fucking pig.'

'I'm not a fucking pig.'

'Not good enough.'

'Okay! Okay!' I raised my hands in a gesture of defeat. 'You want to shoot me, Tony? Get it over with. Do it. Shoot me. Kill me. Stick that big gun in my face, pull the trigger. It'll make you feel better.'

'Think I won't?'

'Think that even if I'm not police, they won't be through the door before my body hits the floor? Your dad's been shot. And they've left to your own devices? They're watching, Tony, waiting for you to slip up. What do you think that guy was over here earlier for?'

He's breathing hard. Spittle erupts between his lips. They look too red against the paleness of his skin. 'You wouldn't lie?'

I drop my hands again 'Jesus Christ! I've never seen a man die before. I saw Neil…I saw him… Even when we killed Ray, or thought we did, we didn't…. I didn't have to see his bloody face!'

He hesitates.

'Ray's trying to make you doubt everything. And he wants me dead too. He knows I'm involved. You said it yourself.'

'You planted the bomb.'

At Tony's insistence. Final proof of my loyalty. Like I'd had a choice. 'I planted the bomb. I let it go off. Think about it. If I'm the police, I might have tried to stop it?'

He lowers the weapon, puts it on the coffee table. Still hesitant, but it allows me the chance to breathe.

'Dunc,' Tony says. 'He mentioned Dunc.' He grabs the phone from the cradle, walks out the room.

I look at the gun on the coffee table. Consider taking it. Ending this. Maybe Ray would thank me. Maybe that's my way out. The endgame. I've been trying to use Tony, but this is too close. I'm walking on the edge.

So what's the plan?

Kill Tony. Save Kat. Jet off to a new life. Leave Crawford and Burke to pick up the pieces? Not unheard of. There was a cop down in London I heard about, who moonlighted as a hitman, only killing people he felt deserved it. When he was found out, he nicked off to places unknown, was never heard from again.

Officially, at least.

Police rumour mill? Myth? Legend? I'd always believed it, myself. Maybe because I wanted to. There was something oddly romantic about the story. An anti-hero doing the wrong things for the right reasons. And getting away with it.

A good way of justifying yourself. Something I'd been looking for ever since I got deeper in than Crawford and Burke had ever expected. So I could end this here and now, with a bullet. One shot. And I deal with a big part of my problem.

He isn't expecting it. Doesn't think I'm capable of it. But am I a killer? Can I be one? I helped with the bomb, but like I told Tony, that was impersonal. Killing from a distance. Besides, he'd made sure I was nice and high beforehand, and if I hadn't played my part, I'd be the one dead, now.

Not that I'm saying I have the moral high ground. I beat the crap out of deadbeats, junkies, jakies all in the name of my cover. But I never killed anyone or went too far. Did just enough that Tony and his dad would trust me.

Could I kill a man like Anthony Scobie? In my head, it seems easy. Justified.

I reach for the gun. My fingers skate across the surface of the weapon. A charge runs down my arm.

I pull back. Change my mind.

Tony comes back down the stairs. Shaking now. Sniffs something right off the back of his hand. 'Dunc's not answering. Fat pillock's either sleeping something off or...' Tony curls his upper lip. Maybe in disgust. Or uncertainty. He doesn't finish the thought. Takes the gun from where left it on the table, hefts it. I don't want to look, but I imagine he's getting hard beneath his jeans. 'This ends tonight. That's how Ray wants it. That's how it's going to be.'

I pull away from Tony. Take a deep breath.

The panic is gone. The fight or flight reflex dulled. The danger now past. My mind starts to make connections it couldn't earlier. Telling me there's something wrong, something I couldn't quite put my finger on. It's been bugging me for a long time, but I haven't been able to put it into words.

And now, in the quiet following the danger of discovery, I'm starting to make connections I couldn't see before.

The story was that Ray betrayed the family. Sold out to Buchan. Tony had presented the trail to prove it. I'd been there. Derek had asked for me to come along, the idea being that I wasn't so emotionally involved, that maybe I'd be able to see the truth.

At the time, I hadn't been able to come up with anything to disprove what Tony claimed to have discovered. It looked like Ray had betrayed his brother and his father. No doubt in anyone's mind.

Yet when I talked to Ray in the hospital, he didn't confirm what Tony had said. The mention of Buchan had confused him more than anything. At the time, I'd figured that for the after-effects of nearly dying. He'd been confused. His memory had got Swiss-cheesed.

But now, things are beginning to click into place. Inconsistencies are creating a new narrative.

I say, 'Your brother didn't betray you.' Tony doesn't react. Just looks at me, lip still curled. 'You knew all along. All that so-called evidence, it was nonsense. A paper trail you created. Complete fakery.'

He licks his lips. No register of emotion. Besides, the only one he knows is anger.

'Why would I do that?' He speaks slow and cautious, fighting back the rush of speech that usually comes out when he's high.

Maybe the shock of my deductions have sobered him up. 'You said it yourself.' Hoping he thinks I'm on his side, that I'm playing the part of the dutiful soldier. At least, the would-be soldier.

'Said what?'

'That your dad, the old ways, they're obsolete. A new world needs a new way and a new plan. And that's you.'

'So why would I kill my brother?'

'He was the reason you couldn't step up. Your dad was an old man. If you wanted to, you could take care of him easily. Not kill him, but maybe brush him aside. But your brother was his muscle. Dad's protection. The source of the old man's power. Take Ray out of the equation, you could move in. I don't know, like, maybe influence the old man. Effect a takeover without fear of reprisal.'

'That's cold, man.'

'Telling me you wouldn't have the balls?'

There's silence for a moment. Have I pushed the wrong way? Hard to tell with men like Anthony when it's the right time to call them out. He could turn, easy. Like pulling the proverbial tiger's tail: one minute it's all a game, then it's teeth, claws, blood, flesh and pain.

'Dangerous fuckin' talk, there.'

I don't say anything.

'You worked it out by yourself?'

'I notice things.'

'Always thought you were cosying up to the old man.'

'Whoever's got the power,' I said. 'Whoever's going to assure my future.'

He smiles. 'Sooner or later, I'd have to make a choice. About you, man. You just fuckin' made it for me. My cousin...' his smile fades. Another mood change. Tony's like the Glasgow weather: you don't know what's coming next, but you can be certain it's probably not sunshine. 'My cousin... love her, you know? She's... Sod it, she's a

124

Scobie. Not in the life, man, but all the same…she's saved my shite on more than one occasion. And she loved you. Like, real love. The whole choirs and angel chorus shite. For a while, anyway.'

'I know,' I say.

'So why'd you let her go? Why choose us and not her? You're not like us, aye? We didn't choose this life. You did.'

I hesitate. He looks at me. 'I don't have family,' I say. 'Mum and Dad dead. No brothers or sister. No uncles or aunts. And then you…you and your dad…you accepted me. In a way I don't know Kat ever could. I didn't stop loving her, but at the same time…' I stop talking. Maybe he thinks I can't keep going. Maybe he thinks I can't come up with a decent excuse.

All I can see is the gun. Slowly, it drops.

He stares at me with blank eyes that make me think of his brother.

Blinks. Is he getting emotional? Over Kat? Or something deeper? An acknowledgement of his own betrayal.

Family is everything to these people, encoded in the Scobie DNA. They would lay down their lives for each other without ever thinking why. That's been one of the reasons it's been tough to break the inner circle. Loyalty is absolute. Blood trumps anything else. Or so they keep telling themselves.

It was easy to believe, of course.

One of the reasons why Ray's apparent defection came as a surprise. Why it provoked such a brutal reaction. Also why I couldn't see Tony's betrayal, even when it was right in front of my face.

Tony. The son. The blood. Planning wholesale betrayal. Probably for a long time. Combine that with the drugs and what I'm convinced is a general undiagnosed psychopathy, and you have someone utterly unpredictable. I don't think even he knows which way he's going to jump next.

He wants to be a leader. Wants people to fall at his feet. He saw what the old man had and wanted to make a play for it. Going against that Scobie herd instinct. Which is why he's getting so cut up over Kat: the only Scobie who never wanted power, who never hurt anyone else. He's making up for the guilt he feels over his own actions. Despite everything, despite what she said when she left, he still cares for her.

Not for who she is, of course. For what she is.

Family.

I say, 'Raymond won't hurt her.'

He shakes his head. 'You don't know him like I do.'

'I know enough. He cares for her like you do.'

'He was the one who got her involved.'

No. She was in the wrong place at the wrong time. Raymond, like Anthony, treasures her innocence, puts her on a pedestal and makes like she's a saint. Because she's the closest any of these men will ever know to innocence. They don't love her. They love the idea of her.

She's a dream girl. A pixie. A mythical creature. No wonder they've always been so protective of her. So understanding of her decision to try and live like any normal citizen.

'He can't hurt her,' I say. 'He won't.'

'If he does,' Anthony says, 'he'll wish he died in that fire.'

Look at those eyes. Pupils wide, the black overtaking the blue. Pure crazy.

I say, 'When this is over, it's you and me, man. No-one will ever hurt her.'

He nods.

I think about the look on his face when they take him down. Wish I'll be around to see it. But I'll be on a plane high above the Atlantic. And Kat will be with me.

And all of this will be fading so fast, we'll think it was a bad dream, a nightmare that lasted most of our lives and then vanished upon waking. Like all nightmares, it would become little more than a dissipated fog of discomfort that holds no real fear when you stop and think about it.

Kat

The markings on the road blur and blend into each other. A long, white line that runs into eternity.

The world seems distant. Sensations are muffled. My hands don't register the touch of the steering wheel. I don't know much pressure I'm applying to the accelerator.

Nothing matters.

Maybe I always accepted that my uncle would die violently. Not at the hands of Ray. But someone would try and murder him eventually. The life he led, not many people ended up dying peacefully. Even taking Arthur Thompson into account, a heart attack was not the way most gangsters went out.

Uncle Derek.

Neil.

I'd been able to accept what happened because of who they were. Push past the shock and accept the situation and accept their deaths as a kind of karma. You don't do bad things without bad things happening to you.

So how to explain Lesley? A girl who spent her life trying to help people? Who didn't deserve what happened?

He shot her in the face.

Ray is a killer. Not a psychopath. But he is not afraid to take another person's life. I keep thinking that he warned her what would happen and she didn't listen. He's a soldier in a never-ending war. He kills for a greater cause. The idea of guilty or innocent doesn't enter into it.

The only question: are you in his way?

I guess I understood that. He warned me. I listened. I'm still alive.

We're heading out towards Newlands, via the M77. Close to the Barrhead Road exit, I get this sick feeling in my stomach and my arms spasm. The car seems to lose weight, lose the heft and control. I blink and imagine crashing through the barriers, flipping over and off the road.

Is this what I want? I take a deep breath, grip the wheel tightly. Try not to cry as I slow down, take the exit too carefully, the cars following me blasting horns as they overtake, letting me know what they think of my abilities.

Ray, in the passenger seat, doesn't react.

He's been quiet since we left Lesley's. All he's done is reload the handgun. Pressing bullets into the clip with the practiced skill of a man who's done it too many times before. As we exit the tunnel, he slams the clip into the gun's butt and then sits back.

'I'm sorry about what happened,' he says.

'You didn't have to kill her.'

'I told her what would happen.'

'No. No, that's not fair. She's not…most ordinary people…'

'I warned her.'

What can I say? What can I do?

Is it my fault?

On Barrhead Road, near the road toll roundabout, I pull over, kill the engine. Shudder, drop my head against the wheel. We sit in the shadow of nearby multis.

'What are you doing?'

'Just kill me,' I say. 'Just do it. I'm dead already, right?'

'I –'

'If you can kill her you can kill me.' Is this what I want?

Maybe.

'No.' Ray speaks with a finality that would at any other time end the conversation.

I raise my head. He's looking at me. In the half-light, he could be Frankenstein's monster, peering out of the darkness. I guess he always was: created by family and circumstance. What he has become is not his own fault. It was all he ever could be. Maybe if people had treated him differently, if he had been raised by

128

another family, if…

If…

If…

Do we have any choice at all in life?

'You know what you are?' I ask.

'Yes.'

'Do you care?'

He doesn't answer.

'What happens if I get out of the car?' I ask. 'What happens if I walk away?'

Recklessness? Bravado?

I can't say for sure. The words are out before I have time to consider them. And I know that I can't take them back.

He doesn't say anything. I take a deep breath, unclick the seatbelt and open the door. He doesn't move. I get out. Close the door. Nothing.

I think that I want him to kill me.

At least that way this will be over.

I walk down Pollockshaws Road. The urge to look back is overwhelming. But I resist. Keep walking. Listening for the footsteps. The click of the trigger.

But I hear nothing.

Is this how it ends?

No bang. Not even a whimper.

Just silence.

There's a guy walking towards me. Dressed in jeans and a dark jacket. A small dog trots just ahead, tugging at her lead. Little mongrel with thick black hair and a relentless enthusiasm. Barks when she sees me. The guy tries to tug at her lead. 'Suzy!'

I can't resist a smile. Always wanted a dog. Don't know why I never got one.

Suzy doesn't pay attention to her owner, starts tugging that lead, trotting on over to me. She's strong, and the guy stumbles with her. Suzy places her front paws on my legs. Her tongue sticks out. I give her head a pat.

I'm still alive. I walked away.

Ray didn't kill me.

Why? Because he couldn't?

But I deserve to die. I'm just like him. Hope that all of this is a bad dream.

Suzy's owner says, 'Really, I'm sorry, she's –' He stops, and I realise what I must look like. 'Are you okay?'

'I'm fine.'

'No,' he says. 'I don't… Is that blood?'

'I'm fine.' He backs off at the aggression. Then sees something over my shoulder. 'Hey there,' talking to someone behind me. 'I think this girl needs –'

It feels like the inside of my brain is on fire. The roar begins intense before it dulls to a deep, aching throb that makes me want to drop to my knees and start crying.

Suzy's owner is gone, and it's only when I look down that I realise he's on the ground, face first. Suzy's bouncing around him, nudging him with her paws and her nose, trying to get a response out of him.

I look up and see Ray.

He leans in to me. 'You asked…what would happen.' His voice sounds muffled. I know that it's the trauma of the gunshot playing havoc with my hearing. All the same, it feels like the world is running away from me again. 'One warning. Only one. You're… family, after all.'

I look at Suzy's owner. At Suzy. Then at Ray.

John

First time I ran for Tony, I thought that I could be working the shortest undercover gig in history.

It wasn't the fear of being caught. Long as I let Crawford know what was happening, he could arrange for the Jam Sandwiches to be rolling elsewhere in the city. The only way I'd find myself in jail would be through my own stupidity.

But I was still afraid. There was no training to prepare me for the reality of a drop without backup. No step-by-step process to follow that would ensure the operation ran like clockwork. I had to endure all the nerves of a first time drop, coupled with the fear that someone knows something they shouldn't. That you've been found out. That the entire enterprise is little more than an elaborate ploy to end your undercover career in the most painful fashion possible.

I knew how the old man treated traitors. I'd seen the autopsy photos.

At our final briefing, I'd jokingly asked Crawford if I could have cyanide pills. Just in case. He hadn't smiled. And not just because I wasn't funny.

The run was simple. Pick up the bag from a third party at a spit-and-sawdust pub over on the Gallowgate. Walk a few streets away, the boozers were segregated by which football team you supported. But this place had no loyalties. To teams, political ideologies or supposed religious affiliation. It was a boozer where the only thing that mattered was money. And not the kind you used to pay your tab.

The girl behind the bar didn't say a word as she poured my pint. No eye contact. She took my money and slammed back the change on the bar. As I turned to find a table, an old duffer at the bar lifted his head and said, 'You're no from round here, son.'

I didn't respond.

The swap came easier than the pint. I finished my drink sitting across the table from a young guy with a noticeable scar running from the bottom of his left ear to just above his mouth. The look in his eyes was hard. Made me think of lifers I'd seen in prison, the kind of who had no idea that there was a safer kind of life out there, who had given up all hope of getting out of the circles of violence and poverty they found themselves in.

He could barely have been twenty years old.

Once we were done, I left the bar, legs shaking. I thought the pint would settle me. Instead all it did was get my heart thumping. I needed to be sharp for this, all I could think about was how fuzzy I'd become. Just one pint, coupled with the adrenaline spike I was in danger of getting sloppy.

I took a deep breath. Steadied myself. Still shaking. Thinking: *what happens if this goes wrong?*

Best-case scenario, I got picked up by cops who didn't know to keep off the drop path, taken in and then we'd have to find a way of getting my story straight so I could get out again. I'd do time for the crime, no question, or it would be obvious that I wasn't all I appeared to be.

But worse than that, what if I gave myself away as a copper to the wrong people? Say the kid noticed something off about me in there, smelled the copper on me?

What if they already knew? What if this was less a test, more of a trap?

Jesus.

I ran across the road, jumped in the car. Hands shaking, I fumbled the key into the ignition. Tried to drive naturally as possible, but my adrenaline levels were spiked, and it was all I could do not to hammer my foot down on that accelerator to increase the rush. There was no back up in this gig. No team nearby waiting to pounce if things went wrong.

Crawford had told me I'd be on my own. This deep, backup and back doors were more danger than safety net.

For the first time since going undercover, I experienced real fear. Sneaking from my belly into my extremities, working its way to the front of my brain. I'd been on the fringes so far, using my connection with Kat to draw myself ever closer to the inner circle. She was an innocent. But the family loved her so much, they took her word as being good as anyone else's.

She loved me, I could be trusted.

Blood is thicker than water.

Aye, and so's porridge.

But the Scobies believed in family. Or at least, paid it constant lip service. Of course the cracks were there. The familial tensions that would fuel Anthony's self-serving betrayal were obvious to an outsider looking to find them. Only proving my own experience correct.

But that belief made my job easier. Sure, at first I had pursued Kat with only the job in mind. But now when I really fell for her, it seemed to ease the minds of her family, as though they sensed the sincerity.

Good for the job. Maybe not so good for me.

A few months after me and Kat moved in together, I started going to the doctors with all sorts of complaints from the minor to the potentially serious. The medicine cabinet at the flat was filled with PeptoBismol, Rennies, medicines for ulcers, and pills I could barely pronounce, never mind remember what they were for. When Kat asked, I told her severe IBS. But it was the double life that had started doing for me. Psychological rather than physical sickness.

And it would only get worse.

That night, my first drop, it was the first time I got that sinking sickness that would only get worse as the months went on. And it seemed insane later, but as I kept driving, the idea that I might shit myself was somehow worse than the terror of being revealed as an undercover copper.

I drove out to a pair of high rises just four minutes from the pub. Like the old Red Road flats, the twins had been a part of Scotland's failed community living experiments. Tall buildings intended as symbols of hope for the post-war world, but soon became reminders of our worst economic failures. The close-together flats designed to create communities instead created fear when unemployment and a wave of drugs invaded these once close communities. The buildings themselves became less aspirational and more claustrophobic. Now they were scheduled for demolition, most of the tenants being rehomed or asked to leave. But there were still a few holdouts, waiting for the bitter end.

The buildings glared down at me. Shadows spread across the street. Grass embankments looked more mud than greenery. Bottle shards and needles glinted in headlights.

Our very own ghettos. Except in Scotland, we've always been equal opportunity about our poor. The poor, the disenfranchised, the lost, it didn't matter where you came from, once you ended up here people tended to forget who you were.

I made sure the car was locked, kept looking back as I walked to the front entrance of the block. I walked past what had once been a reception area, the watchman's booth locked and abandoned for a long time. The interior smelt faintly of sweat and piss. Half-arsed graffiti daubed the walls. The lift was, of course, out of order.

On my way up the stairs, the graffiti became more legible:

FukPedrofiles

Kimbo is a lesbo dike

And more.

Time was, I worked the beat in places like this. The sergeant who trained me up used to say that when the graffiti was that poor, there was no hope left. Right enough, it was hard to spot a future Banksy among the scrawls.

The building was quiet, except for the distant hum of TV shows from somewhere I couldn't identify. I kept looking over my shoulder, expecting someone to jump me. When I came to places like this in uniform, most people would back off. Now, I was naked.

An intruder. I stood out. With no protection. Carrying a bag stuffed with product whose street value I could only guess at.

On the top floor, I found the door I was looking for, knocked hard. The man who answered wasn't quite what I expected. For a start, he was half-naked, his lower half only just covered by the fluffiest towel I'd seen outside of a *Malmaison*.

'Aye?'

I held up the bag. 'Anthony sent me. You're Pete?'

He shook his head. 'Wayne.'

I nodded. He stepped back. 'So come in, if you're going to.' That odd accent – the mix of his Polish parents and his Glasgow upbringing – puzzled me the first time I heard it.

He closed the door behind me. The sound it made had a strange finality. The heavy stone door of a tomb closing on a man who was still alive. No going back now. No chucking it all in and walking away.

My insides scraped worse than ever. I'd be shitting out razor blades later.

I was still holding the bag when we walked into the living room. Big screen telly, maybe forty inches, another guy lounging around. This one smaller, wearing a shellsuit with the top unzipped. His white chest was hairless and barely defined. He turned and nodded. 'Seen this?' he said.

I didn't recognise the image paused on the screen.

'Fuckin' amazing,' Wayne said. 'Baltimore, man, there's a place a dude could earn a buck.'

'Speak like that again,' Pete said, 'I'll rip your fucking tongue out.' He looked at me and smiled. 'Seriously, it was bad enough when he had an addiction to 24, kept talking about going dark and giving me ETAs on all kinds of things, like even how long he'd take to shite.'

Wayne chuckled. Pete didn't look amused.

I tried to look uninterested. All business. Do the deal. Get out.

Pete said, 'Wait here,' and left the room.

Wayne said, 'Want something? Drink? Got some brews.'

'No,' I said. 'It's fine.'

He smiled, stood up. Maybe five-seven or eight, he was a few inches shorter than me, stood with the kind of straight back that told me how aware he was of his own height. He came close to me. 'You're with Kat, then?'

I didn't say anything. But I couldn't stop myself stiffening up. The idea that they knew anything about gave me the chills. All I'd been given was a pair of names and an address.

He said, 'You know she's not involved in any of this?'

'Aye.'

'So what the fuck're you doing here?'

'I needed the money,' I said. 'Business isn't doing as well as it could… You know how it is right now. And…and I need the money.'

'Why?'

'What do you care?'

'Kat's like a wee sister, you know? We're not blood, not like her and Tony, but we're close. I just don't want her…involved…with the wrong man.'

'I love her.'

'Easy to say.'

'When it's true.'

He nodded. For a moment I thought he might nut me one. Braced myself for the impact from the heavy looking forehead. But what he did was take a step back. 'I'd think twice how deep you go, man. You don't strike me being right for this. Know what I mean? You're straight, got that scent about you.'

I wanted to smile then.

I'm not a citizen. I'm a copper. A copper worthy of winning a fucking Oscar.

'I can handle myself. You know how it is, though, you love your girl, you have to love her family, too.'

'Tell me about it,' said a voice from the door. I turned to see Pete, now dressed in jeans and a grey t-shirt that fit snugly on his body-builder chest. 'And this bawbag's family are hard to love.'

I relaxed. There was a feeling like I was visiting with friends. They weren't out to screw me. Of course, I knew their reputation. If I messed them about, they'd show me what being fucked over was all about. Pete came over, passed me a new bag. Lighter colours. It weighed me down, heavier, it seemed than the drugs. 'This is deep as you want to go, bud. Trust me.'

'I'm a big boy.'

'Sure you are,' said Wayne. 'But like I said, first person we're watching out for is Kat. Always will be.'

'Same with me,' I said. 'Same with me.'

•   •   •

First person I'm watching out for.

Kat.

Not me.

It had been a lie, then. First person I was watching out for was me, because I didn't want to die. And it was soon exposed as a lie when I got deeper and deeper involved in Tony's world, going against everything Kat wanted.

•   •   •

I had a flat in Partick. Rent covered by the job, but all the cash came through back channels so no-one could trace it.

The place was decent enough, but most of the décor consisted of gifts from Kat. She'd been the one to put her mark on the place. Left to my own devices, what I'd have had would have been best described as 'Spartan'. Which might have been too generous.

'Do you actually own anything?'

Wayne looking at the bookshelves and the pictures. Pete was on the sofa, arm stretched over the back, looking like he owned the place.

When I'd answered the door, I'd almost collapsed when I saw them. Thinking, *at least it's not Ray.*

'We need to talk.'

Words you don't want to hear.

And now they were in my front room, not really talking, just looking around like they were trying to formulate a way of explaining why they were here.

'The old man's confused,' Wayne said, still looking at the shelves.

'About what you really want,' Pete added.

'Have to say, we are too. I remember you coming to our place the first time, talking big about she was the most important thing in your life.'

'She is.'

'Yeah?'

Pete said, 'The old saying? You love something, let it go?'

'Something like that.'

Wayne laughed. Turned to face me. 'You're a bastard, you know that?'

I didn't say anything. Met his gaze. Gave nothing away.

'We're all bastards,' Wayne said. 'But we came here to tell you, you made a choice and now you're in. All the way, man.'

Pete nodded. Slow. 'All the way.'

'What we're saying is your first mistake was breaking her heart. The old man, he takes family seriously. Anyone else...' He stopped there, not finishing the thought. 'But the fact is that you're family too now. In a different way.'

'Like us,' Pete said.

Wayne finally turned to face me. 'You think it's hard being the nephew-in-law? I mean, all he expected of you then was to be a stand-up guy when it came to Kat. Those favours, they were just, you know, little treats thrown your way, a little sideline to help you provide for her by doing something for him. But now...now things are different.' He shakes his head. 'We just kind of figured we'd pop by and let you know.'

There was a part of me swelled up then. A little inner pride that knew I was another step closer to breaching the inner circle.

I think I still believed in the operation, then.

Pete giggled on the sofa. 'Oh, boy,' he said. 'You ain't seen nothing yet.'

• • •

'Fuck sakes, man! Get out the way!'

The way Tony drives, it's like he knows they're out there. The police. He knows they're following him. And maybe they are. But not for the reasons he thinks. He's weaving between traffic on the carriageway with no regard for the speed limit.

Tony's paranoid at the best of times, but right now he's running on powder and adrenaline. More importantly, fear. Of his own brother.

'Anyone who can follow this,' he says, skipping through Guns N Roses tracks on the stereo, 'deserves to catch me.'

I don't say anything.

He's not that good, but I don't think there's anyone really following us. More than Tony, I know what I'm looking for, and there's no sign of cars that belong to cops or anyone driving in any way that marks them out as trying to remain hidden. All the same, if he keeps this up, some innocent wee traffic cop's likely to spot us, play have-a-go-hero. And then where are we going to be?

As long as this remains contained, there's a chance everything will work out. When you start bringing innocent people into it, that's when things get nasty.

'Fat prick,' Tony mutters. 'Fat fuckin' prick...'

Meaning Dunc.

We're on our way over to Dunc's place. After Ray's phone call, Tony's determined to end all of this, and fast. He's already called Wayne and Pete, told them to meet us there. Ray wants everyone together. In one place. And Tony figures that if they play along, that's the best way to bring his brother out of hiding.

'Try him again,' Tony says.

'Look, Tony –'

'Do it!'

Every two minutes he has me calling Dunc. Trying to raise him from whatever pit he's crawled into. But there's no response, and I have to wonder if Ray's not yanking our chains. But I'm not going to mention that to Tony. No way. He's on edge as things are.

Besides, I'm just along for the ride.

To Tony, I'm simply cannon fodder. He gets the chance, he'll put me in the way of a bullet that's meant for him.

I dial the number again. Get the answer machine. Leave another message. When I hang up, Tony looks at me, his eyes hard. Like all this is my fault.

And in his own way, I guess he's right.

Kat

We park down the road from Dunc's place. When I turn off the engine, Ray looks at me, as though I should be saying something. When I don't speak, he just grunts and gets out the car. I join him. What choice do I have? We are bound. By blood.

We walk to the front door. His left leg moves strangely. His body is shutting down. Piece by piece. Watching it happen is an odd experience. Is he aware of it at all?

Still, there's enough of him working to get the job done. Force of will keeps him on the move. He cannot leave the job unfinished.

Ray knocks hard. When the door opens, Dunc doesn't look surprised. Steps back and lets us inside. As if he's expecting us. Doesn't say a word.

In the front room, Ray tells me to sit down. Remains standing.

I take in the room. Heavy fabrics, dark wood coffee tables and units. DVD cases disguised as hardback books. The kind of thing people thought was sophisticated in the '80s.

Dunc says, 'They're coming over.'

'Good.'

'I can't believe this.'

Ray says nothing.

Dunc walks over to a small oak table set out with decanters and glasses, pours himself a whisky. Offers Ray, who shakes his head. Dunc raises the bottle in my direction, arches his heavy eyebrows in a question. Normally I wouldn't touch the stuff, but after this evening, a little bit couldn't hurt. What, they're going to arrest me for drink driving when this is done?

It tastes as rough as I expect, burns a little going down. But at least I can feel it.

I say, 'Earlier, at the wake, you were trying to tell me to get out.'

Dunc nods. Collapses into the large leather armchair near the window. He's an old man, but right now he looks ancient. His large frame seems incapable of holding its own weight – just one moment away from collapsing completely into a congealed mass of flesh.

'None of this should have happened,' he says. 'Least of all...' He gestures towards me expansively. 'You should never have come home.'

'Family,' I say.

'You're all the same. Touch of the old bugger's madness.'

Ray isn't sitting down. He isn't drinking. He's standing there, watching us.

'I still don't understand,' I say.

Dunc laughs. 'Your cousin is what happened. Anthony. Always a bad 'un. Tried to tell your uncle that, but he'd never hear a word against either of his boys.'

'Except me,' Ray says.

Dunc looks down at the floor. Ashamed. But I don't know what of. Ray says, 'Tony always wanted...Dad's power. I was in...his way. He was scared. I knew that. I was bigger. Could always fight back. Tony's always been...a wee...scaredy-cat prick.'

Dunc snorts. Maybe it's meant to be a laugh. Sounds like he's trying to dislodge something. 'Jesus, that's putting it mildly.'

'So what happened?'

'Tony told them...I was working...with Buchan,' Ray says. 'But...not true...is it?' He looks at Dunc. The old man shrinks in on himself. Shame? Fear?

'No, it's not. Never was.'

'Someone was, though.'

Dunc shakes his head. Glances at me, and I swear he's about to burst into tears. His skin is purple, and his eyes are watery, blood-shot. I wonder how much of that whisky he's already had. 'Your uncle was getting old and desperate. Tony had seen it for a while, that he was losing his touch. We all knew it. But he was the old man. Trouble was, if he lost it then it was his son took over.'

I say, 'Tony.'

'Never hand...power to me,' Ray says. 'The freak.'

Dunc mutters, 'He wasn't wrong,' and then seems to remember where he is, looks up at Ray with wide eyes.

But Ray either doesn't hear or doesn't care.

'I figured I had to make a choice,' Dunc says. 'What I did was approach Buchan.'

Ray shakes his head. He won't look right at Dunc.

'Derek couldn't see past Tony being his son. But anyone with any brains was going to look to Buchan after Derek was gone,' Duncan says.

'But you were stupid,' Ray says. 'You got caught.'

'Aye.' He barely even whispers the word.

I begin to understand. Tony was the one who caught Duncan in his act of betrayal. And used the evidence he had on the old man to frame his brother, get him out of the picture. Smarter move than most people might give him credit for.

But that wasn't the whole story.

'Ray came to me two days ago,' Dunc says. 'Your ex, our shiny new recruit, he's a cop, you know that? Tried to get Ray to turn against the family. Covered up his survival in the explosion. Threatened him.'

But Ray wouldn't turn. Doesn't take a genius to figure that out. He'd kill them for the betrayal, but he'd never turn them into the cops. You don't involve outsiders. Especially the boys in blue.

I say, 'I didn't know.' Except maybe I did. On some level. John's behaviour had been increasingly strange over the last few weeks we were together. Had he given something away? Had I just pretended not to notice? Wanting, on some level, to finally give in to my desire for a normal life, turn my family in without actually seeming to do anything?

The human mind is a strange thing. How many decisions do we make without consciously considering them? How often are we motivated by impulses we never even notice?

Ray says, 'He's dead too. John. The turncoat.' He smiles. His face seems to crack. The grin is a monstrous leer.

He's a death machine. A monster.

'Don't feel sorry...for John,' Ray says. 'He's no...innocent.'

None of us are. 'I never felt sorry for him,' I say.

There's the sound of a car engine outside, slowing down, slowly cutting out.

Dunc says, 'That'll be them.'

Ray nods. 'It ends. Now.'

Part of me wants to ask if I can pull the trigger when Ray presses the gun to John's head. It takes me a moment to realise I don't feel bad about thinking it.

Nature. Nurture. Whatever.

Once a Scobie, always a Scobie.

No matter how much you try to deny it.

John

We pull up outside Dunc's house.

Tony kills the engine. We sit for a moment. Perfectly still. Zen. I look at the house.

Lights on downstairs, orange, slipping through cracks in heavy curtains. The two stories enough for a family of four, maybe even five, but now belonging to one lonely man rattling around in there. When his wife left and the kids finally grew up, he refused to move. This was his house. He'd sweated for it. He was keeping it.

Tony pulls the gun from the glove box. Checks the chamber, looks at me and grins. 'Just in case,' he says. 'Fat boy's getting twitchy, you know. Can't trust him like you used to.' He opens the door. 'Can't trust anyone these days.'

I get out, shiver as the rain hits me. Dark's coming in, and the temperature's plummeted fast.

Tony sends me up front. I knock hard on the door. Wait while he lingers a few steps behind and to the left. He's not daft.

When Dunc answers the door, unarmed, Tony says, 'Bloody turncoat,' and barges past, shoving the fat man out his way. I stomp after him. Dunc's deflated. Knows that this is the end. His eyes are red-rimmed and I catch a whiff of something strong from him.

Tony walks through to the front room, pulls up short so that I almost walk into the back of him.

I need a moment to take in the scene.

Fat Dunc's living room is large, with bay windows that face out onto the front garden. The room is subtly lit from table lamps, the light absorbed by the dark colouring of the furniture and the wallpaper. A false fire sits in one wall, fake flames flickering gently.

But all of that's expected.

What's unusual is someone sitting in one of the armchairs. Back straight, expression neutral, eyes staring straight ahead, deliberately not looking at anything. And especially not at me.

Kat.

She looks tired. Blood on her clothes. I hope to hell that none of it belongs to her. But she's alive.

She's alive.

Tony hesitates just a second too long. Enough to allow his brother to step out from behind the door, press a gun to his head.

Ray's looking bad. Worse than I remember. Literally a dead man walking. Straight out of a George Romero movie. Skin washed out, blood drained from his face. Eyes sinking into their sockets, the whites now an off-yellow and road-mapped by red. Crooked, stooped over, unsteady. Even if he doesn't feel pain, he has to know that something is very, very wrong.

'How it ends,' Ray says.

'With a bang,' says Tony, resigned, with the sullen air of a teenager. He drops the gun, then kicks it away, skiting it across the thick carpet. The weapon winds up at Dunc's feet. The fat man looks down. Doesn't react. He's past trying to fight back. Old, unfit and tired.

'You're a hard one to kill,' Tony says to his brother.

'You're…just not that good.'

'Dad said you were a monster. You know that? He was scared of you. When you were a wee boy, you never laughed. That's what he said, you never laughed. That fucking terrified him.'

'I know.'

'I thought you'd have killed her,' Tony says, nodding at Kat. 'But you were always a sentimental prick.'

'This is…between us.'

'Aye. That it is. Goodnight, Gracie.' Tony laughs.

I look at Dunc.

He's not moving. The gun's at his feet, and he's not moving.

All I have to do now is keep my cool. Choose my moment.

It can end here. Three men dead. No-one to know what I did. Kat still alive. Maybe I can talk to her. Maybe she'll understand

145

why I lied to her. Looking at her, though, it's hard to tell anything about what she's thinking. If she's thinking at all.

She's alive. No question. Unharmed, I'm sure. Banged up, perhaps, but no more than you might expect. That blood on her clothes, it's not hers. I don't care whose it is, but it's not hers.

Thing is, though, she's sitting perfectly still. Not moving.

Look at the brothers just inside the living room door. One with the gun to the other's head. Happy bastard families.

When Ray's done with Tony, he'll kill me. Not just because I helped set the bomb, but because I'm a copper, too.

Bang, bang, you're dead.

I've seen dead bodies. But only ever the aftermath. The tragedy about being a copper is that you're always reacting; showing up after the fact. I've seen the terrible things people can do to each other, but never this close, this raw. Never felt hatred manifest itself as some tangible, physical presence. Never had my muscles tense so hard I'm worried they might just snap.

Never seen a man's brains blown all over a richly expensive carpet.

There's been enough violence. Enough death, I'm not so far gone I can just let this happen. Even if Tony fucking well deserves it. Even if it would be doing the world a favour to let a man like him die.

There's a difference between what's good and what's right. Between what you think should be done and what your conscience will allow.

Aye, fine time to become a philosopher.

Ray has his gun pressed up hard against the side of his brother's head. His trigger finger's tightens. When you enter a heightened state, when adrenaline starts to course through your body, you sometimes see things you would otherwise miss. Little details stand out. There's a reason in cop movies that they slow down the action when a fire fight begins or when a murderer enters the room.

Little things. Details.

Ray's knuckles whitening as he prepares to kill his brother.

Tony's lips curving up to the left in this jagged half smile, like he knows he has nothing to fear. The original cocky bastard.

He expects to be saved.

The universe will not let Tony Scobie died. Not when he engineered the death of his father. Not when he is this close to getting everything he ever wanted.

He knows it. The smarmy bollocks.

I should let him die. Show him that he's mortal after all. All I need to do is wait. One second. That's all.

But I can't.

For all I've done. For all the bad moves I've made over the last few years. For all that I've compromised myself since getting close to these men, I can't let him die.

Can't watch it happen.

I still believe in something. Some kind of order. Some kind of morality.

Why else would I be here? Pretending to be the knight in shining armour. Endangering myself to save one person who doesn't care if I live or die. Who probably hopes I wind up taking a bullet for all that I put her through.

I don't even think about it. I barrel forward, head down, knock my left shoulder into Tony's back as I reach up with my right hand to grip Ray's wrist, twist his grip on the gun.

Suicidal?

Sod it. I'm dead either way.

The explosion from the gun reverberates through my body. My bones vibrate. The skin on my hand burns. Bubbles and blisters. I let go of Ray. The spark from inside the barrel is in my field of vision. My eyes burn. The world turns a dull white, and floating transparent bubbles bob around inside my head.

I land heavy, right side hammering on top of Tony as he wallops to the floor. Something snaps, and I wonder if it's his rib or mine. I roll off him, stay on my back, breathing hard, ragged, like I'm sucking in shards of ice.

I can't see a thing. I close my eyes. Squeeze them tight. Maybe it's just a temporary thing. I pray it is. But even if God's there, why would he listen to me when I never listened to him?

There's a low, constant roar in my head. No other noise. I could be floating face-up in the middle of the ocean, the sun beating down on me. Lost, weightless, far away from anything that matters.

That's where I want to be. Where I've always wanted to be. Somewhere still. Quiet. Undisturbed.

As a child, I'd play with the other kids, but I was always happiest leaving them behind, going back home, shutting myself in my room and just sitting there in the quiet.

The quiet is bliss.

The gentle roar soothing.

Is this heaven?

I doubt it.

• • •

'It's a simple question.'

No, it really wasn't. Maybe to her it was simple. But to me, it was the most complex question in the world.

Was I with her for her?

Or her family?

Indecision. Uncertainty. Something in my brain tripped. Made me freeze up.

'That's the answer, then.'

We were in a bar near the Mitchell Library. Place where we went on our first date. The kind of bar that's cool enough it doesn't need to have its name on its door. Named for one of those hip writers had their day in the '50s and '60s. The beat generation. She'd brought me here deliberately, I guess, to try and spark a response out of me. Symbolism. Trying still to rekindle something. But this was our last chance to salvage anything.

And it was too late. Maybe we both knew.

'I really thought you were different.' She looked at me over a glass of wine she hadn't touched since sitting down. I took a slug from my pint in a vain need to do something, anything. Because I knew that whatever I said, I either screwed her or I screwed the operation. Both outcomes were equally bad.

From a personal point of view.

'All my life, it's been men who wanted to get close to my uncle, get a taste of the gangster life. You were supposed to be different. There was no face with you, no deception.'

I sat there and took every word. Offering no defence. No excuse. The job demanded it. That had been made clear to me: I was getting too close to my target, delaying the necessary work of entangling myself into Derek Scobie's life. Starting with small financial favours, slowly making my way into more criminal activities.

The way in had been through Kat. Problem was, that was where the lines blurred between me and my cover. Between who I was pretending to be and who I really was.

Don't fall for the target.

Aye, great advice. Great bloody advice.

'I'm sorry,' was the best I could manage.

She'd already told me she's leaving, got a transfer to a hospital somewhere up near Shetland. Looking for a quieter life, and one away from all that being a Scobie in Glasgow entails, whether you're on the right side of the law or not.

'That's really it?'

I took another drink.

'It was good,' she said.

'It was,' I agreed.

'Bastard,' she said. First time I ever heard her swear. The only time, now that I think about it. She took the business of being the only decent member of her family seriously, although sometimes

I wondered if it was that which screwed her up, made her toss and turn at night, was responsible for the indistinct sounds she made as she slept restlessly and in fits and starts.

When she left, her glass remained full.

I finished my pint. Called her cousin to tell him what had happened.

• • •

The bubble bursts. The ocean recedes.

Someone's hands are on my shoulders. A voice yells somewhere beyond a locked door. I can't make out the words. They blend into long stream of gibberish.

I blink. The light is gone. There's a stippling at the edge of my vision.

Tony's the one gripping my shoulders, pulling me up and off the carpet so that his face is inches from my own. Another situation, it might be romantic, but his features are contorted with feral anger, and I can smell the stale stench of his breath, feel the hot spittle land on my skin as he yells at me:

'–up, you tosser! Get up and get your arse in gear!'

I hustle my shoulders and he backs off. I bum it away from him and sit up straight. I think I might vomit, but thankfully swallow the urge.

My head is too small. My skull has contracted. There's a sharp pain in my side, and when I move, I breathe out fast and get this deeper stippling on the right of my vision.

I lie back.

Someone else is beside me. On his knees. He puts heavy hands on my body. Presses down where the pain is.

I scream.

Fat Dunc says, 'You'll live.'

I don't feel like it. What does he know? Is he a doctor, now?

Tony says, 'Get him the fuck up, then.'

With Dunc's help I struggle into a chair.

150

'Where's Ray?' I ask. 'Kat?' My voice sounds strange. Like I've got a bad cold that's ripped my throat raw.

'Aye,' Tony says. 'You may well fucking ask, my son.'

Kat

I'm going to die.

I'm going to die.

I'm going to die.

. . .

I'm flying.

The night air breezes against my face. I swoop through the dark. Free.

Free from everything.

I can see the city below. I think to myself that I won't miss it. I just need to fly higher. And higher.

I don't have to go back to what I used to have. Don't have to think about anything. All I have to do is close my eyes and fly.

. . .

'Kat?'

Mum's talking close to my ear, the way she used to when I was ill. Five or six years old, running a fever, she'd sit beside me in bed and tell me stories. Her lips right next to my ear gently speaking in a soft rhythm that calmed my breathing, made me feel safe.

'Kat?'

I try to speak, but my throat is closed. I can taste blood.

'It's all right, Kat. It's okay. There's nothing to be afraid of.'

Am I crying? I don't know.

'I'm always here, honey. Always. Beside you. Looking out for you.'

'I know.'

'The only good one was Ray. You know that, right? That they made him what he was? That he was always different.'

'He's a killer.'

'A wee boy pulling wings off flies. Doesn't understand that they feel things.'

'What's to stop him taking my wings?'

'He'd never do that, baby. Not Ray. He told me. He told me he'd always look out for you. Always.'

• • •

I open my eyes. Back seat of a car. The engine rumbles gently. But that's not what woke me. It's the way the car slides about the road, like whoever's up front can't control the wheel. It slips through their hands. Easy enough done when your hands are slick with blood.

I try to move and something in my abdomen protests. A dull kind of pain. At first, simply insistent. But then I push it too far and it becomes this jagged icicle sticking inside my gut. I cry and fall back to how I was before.

The pain eases. The sweat on my forehead cools.

In the front seat, Ray says, 'Shhhh, shhhh,' and doesn't look back. Too busy focussing on the road.

'Where are we going?' I ask.

'Your friend...said it. Hospital.'

'Hospital?'

'Wasn't supposed...to happen.'

'What?'

But I know what he's talking about.

Like thinking back over a movie half-watched in the dark. Remembering fragments. Moments. Piecing together the idea that something larger had happened. Filling in the blanks.

• • •

Ray had a gun to Tony's head.

Ready to kill his brother.

But he hesitated. Because unlike Tony, Ray believed in everything he had been told as a child. Everything that his father had said. He truly believed that in some special connection among our family.

But he had already killed his father. I can only imagine the strength of will that required. And now his brother? Could he really do it?

I watched, observing from this space inside my head where I was completely safe. Like I wasn't really there at all. Maybe in the cinema or curled up on front of the TV with the lights off.

Tony had come through the door after Dunc. That was when Ray made his move, stepped out, held the weapon against Tony's skull and told him to drop his own gun. Just behind them, still in the main hall, I could see John.

John.

Looking tired. Hair messed up, skin pale, eyes wide. Dressed the same as at the funeral, but now his tie was loose and the top few buttons of his shirt were undone. Another time, I might have thought he looked rakish, a little sexy in that kind of messed-up way. But looking at him then, I felt disgust.

Not just at him. More than a touch of self-loathing in there too.

After all, I'd been the one idiotic enough to fall for his lies. Believing everything he told me. Wide-eyed, innocent, *stupid* girl. Oh, I always knew he was lying, at least a little. Boys always lie. I'd worked that out a long time ago. There's always some little thing they don't tell you, or they exaggerate.

John.

The bastard. The cop. The liar.

His eyes focused on me, as though trying to figure whether I was alive or dead. Maybe it had been hard for him to tell. I hadn't said a word since he entered. Was just sitting there. Breathing in and out, observing everything from that little place inside my head where I could say and think and hate whatever I wanted.

He was still as I was.

And then he moved. Like we were playing musical statues and someone had just turned the music up.

No warning. No indication. He just charged. Shoved Tony forward and reached to grab Ray's gun arm. Maybe he thought he could wrestle the gun from Ray's grip. Maybe he really thought he stood a chance.

I thought he was many things, but I'd never have imagined delusional was one of them.

At least he had the element of surprise.

I watched what happened from the little place inside my head. If I could have, I'd have been eating popcorn.

Ray's gun arm swung up. John hung from it for a second, like a child holding onto a tree branch. His feet might even have left the floor. I figured he was trying to use his weight to knock Ray off balance. Dumb move.

Ray's finger, the one which had already curled into the trigger guard, twitched. I watched it happen. Saw the tiny, imperceptible movement and knew what was coming.

I thought about Lesley. The surprise on her face. The way the dog walker had simply dropped out of my line of sight.

The gun went off.

For just a moment, I thought John had been shot. The gun had been near the side of his head. It was possible he'd been grazed, maybe had his skull drilled.

He let go of Ray's arm and fell on top of Tony. Bounced off my cousin, landed on the floor and let loose this little breath like an exclamation point at the end of a sentence.

That was when I felt the heat at my side. Like someone had spilled tea on my top and it had soaked through, finally touching against the cool of my skin.

I moved.

Finally.

My hand reaching to where I felt the gentle heat and the wet.

Not tea. Thicker. Heavier. I craned my neck. Looked down at myself.

•   •   •

I'd been shot.

The bullet digging deep into my abdomen. Hadn't felt a thing until I realised what had happened.

Me and Ray, bonded by more than family now. Both of us with a bullet inside, bound by the creeping sense of our own mortality.

When it hit me, that's when events stuttered, like a film with scenes and frames randomly dropping out. I remember crying out. Being lifted bodily. Hearing screams and threats that ripped through the air.

And then the flying.

My mother's voice. And now...

Here, in the back of a car. Ray driving me to the hospital. Wondering: is this how it ends?

I pull myself up, both hands grabbing at the front seats and pulling myself forward so that I can speak to him. The effort tears the skin in my side. If I move too much I'll just unravel like a soft toy with bad stitching.

'Is this it?'

Ray says nothing.

'Is this it? You take me to hospital? You know that it's a risk, don't you? That if you drop me off, they'll try and stop you from leaving too?'

'Maybe.'

'Did you kill him?'

'I couldn't let...you...die.'

'Why? You said it yourself, you'd kill me if I got in your way.'

He doesn't say anything, just keeps watching the road. I turn my head to look at him in the rear view mirror. He's pale, and his breathing is getting worse. There's a strange whistling sound every time he breathes out.

He looks worse than I remember.

What happened in that house? Why am I still alive?

'Did you kill him?'

'There was… I…you were…shot. I couldn't…'

'Yes,' I say. 'You could.'

He pulls over to the side of the road, slams on the brakes. We clunk against the rise of the pavement. I lose my balance, twist to the right. Scream in agony as I aggravate the hole in my side.

Jesus, is the bullet in there? Scraping against my internal organs?

I can visualise it. I can see it. The thought make me nauseous, but I hold it down. Same way I'm holding down the horror and overwhelming panic.

Ray turns in the seat. He looks at me as I stay perfectly still, trying to suck breath into my lungs.

'Can't let you die.'

'You told me all that mattered was revenge. That hasn't changed.' My voice is tight. It hurts to speak. A cold, white kind of pain.

He hesitates. I speak through the hurt. 'You killed my best friend. And a man I never met before. Without blinking. Because you know that Tony deserves to die. And you wanted me to understand too.'

I'm light-headed. Losing blood. Possibly delirious. The little part of me that coolly remembers all the training at nursing college tries to tell me that this is a bad idea. I'm going to regret this.

But after all I've seen, I know there's only one way this evening can end.

I'm a Scobie, after all. Much as I try to play the good girl, to live up to my mother's expectations, her double standards, I know what I am. If there's a gene for badness, it's there inside me somewhere, the family inheritance. Why not embrace it? Stop running away from it. Your inheritance. Turn and be honest about who and what you are. Admit that even if you suppress it, the Scobie

156

genes are there, in your blood. You can run away and look out at oceans and pretend you're normal all you like, but in the end you're just like them. Somewhere, deep down.

'Tony deserves to die,' I say, 'More than I deserve to live.'

John

Fat Dunc wheezes.

He's screwed and he knows it. But he's still trying to do what he can to change the situation.

His act – patching me up, making sure the rib was just cracked and not completely broken – was little more than an attempt to make us think he was on our side.

Too little. Too late.

Fat Dunc's children flew the nest a long time ago. His wife followed suit, leaving Dunc to rattle around in this veritable mansion all by himself. The place is thick with memories like dust. Most of them, I imagine, bad.

I wonder what he was like in the old days. What kind of man he used to be that everyone was so scared of. This was the man that Ray learned his trade from. This was the man used to rule the streets of Govan. And now he's a quivering mess. Afraid of dying.

But how long has it been since he lived?

'Tell me when it happened,' Tony says. 'Tell me when my arsehole of a brother got to you.'

Dunc shakes his head. 'I betrayed him. And your old man.'

'Oh, Jesus,' Tony says, and laughs 'Bit late to worry about that, Dunc.'

There's something between the two of them that I haven't seen before. A palpable tension. A guilt that Dunc wants to share, but that Tony could never feel.

Hard to think of Tony feeling anything. Textbook sociopath.

How'd he get that way? Nature or nurture? And what about his bastard brother?

'I thought you were a visionary,' Tony says. 'Thought you had your old balls back.'

'Balls? I had any kind of testicles left, I'd never have trusted you in the first place, you entitled wee prick.'

Tony laughs.

I make the connections in my head.

Tony's plan to take over from his father took more than just brass balls. Took cunning, too. Not Tony's strong suit. His idea of subtlety was a pool cue to the back of the head or a sharp knife across the throat. But this play, setting up Ray to look like he'd betrayed the family, playing a long fucking game to get the old man into a position of weakness, it didn't feel right.

It would take a subtler mind to come up with this kind of plan.

An older mind, perhaps. One with maturity. And patience.

I look at Dunc. The former king-of-the-walk, now an overweight joke to the new generation, a faded memory to the old. What did he have left? Nothing, except an empty house and a feeling that he'd been left behind. Close as him and the man were, when Neil came along – younger, sharper more willing to play the toadie – Dunc became a third wheel. He was the old, trusted family pet, kept around out of sentimentality rather than necessity. No-one wanted to put him down, but no-one really wanted him around, either.

No wonder he'd been tempted by any overture from Buchan. The East Side King, as he's known, always wanted a slice of the Scobie business. And Dunc had all the inside gossip. Bringing along the heir apparent, that would have just been the icing on the cake. Dunc would have been welcomed with open arms.

And then everything went to shite.

Did he intend for Ray to die? How did it feel when the big bastard showed up still alive, hell-bent on revenge against those who had tried to kill him? Why didn't Ray just kill Dunc, same as every other bastard? Did Dunc somehow persuade Ray that he'd never intended for any of this to happen?

Dunc was no longer a hard man. He was a scared old bastard twisting any which way: a snake trying to escape a trap. All he's got to save him now is that he had the presence of mind to grab up Tony's gun when the shooting finally started and fire off shots at Ray, the unkillable bastard.

'But you did trust me,' Tony says. 'You trusted me to lead the family and the business forward into the new fucking millennium. You trusted me to listen to all the advice that the old man didn't want any more. You trusted me to have the balls to give you everything you wanted.'

Dunc's slumped in an armchair. Old, tired, ready to admit defeat. No fight in him. He lost that decades earlier.

'And then you betrayed me.'

Dunc finally looks up.

'My brother comes back from the dead, and you decide that to switch sides yet again? No wonder my dad locked you out. How could he trust you? No principles. You overweight sack of shite. You're a hoor – unable to shag just one guy and let it be.'

'I didn't… What we did…to your brother…it was wrong. It wasn't –'

'Attack of the conscience now, eh? You bloated bag of bollocks.'

I'm holding Tony's gun. Glad of that fact, because I dread to think what would happen to Dunc if the crazy bastard yelling in his face had a weapon.

'You're a liability,' Dunc says. 'Like all your generation. We gave you everything, and what happened was you turned into psychopaths. All of you.'

'Yeah?'

'And, yeah, the coked-up bawbags shall inherit the Earth.'

'So why'd you agree to back my play with Buchan?'

Dunc shifts in the seat. Doesn't seem scared any more. Looking directly at Tony. There's still an air of the dusty old corpse about him. But he's not scared. There's something about him that seems to have forgotten the terror. He's simply accepted where he is.

No matter what he does, he's dead. If Tony doesn't kill him here, then it's like Ray will.

For Fat Dunc, it's all over. His glory days are long gone. He is now nothing more than a fat man trapped in a room with two men he betrayed.

He is a relic.

And he no longer needs to be afraid.

'Why'd I agree to back your play, son? Because I was scared. Not of you, you wee shite, but the world. Everything's changed. I've got old. Fat. Out of touch. My kids hate me. My wife's a distant memory, except for the sodding money she keeps taking.' He sits forward. 'I used to be somebody, son. Before your mum and dad knew they had a mistake on their hands, I was the man who scared the shite out of everyone who knew me. I was the hard bastard, hard-nut cock of the bloody walk. You think you know hard, you don't know the fucking meaning of the word. And I wanted all of that back. Your dad still had it all. And I wanted it. If I could have killed him myself and taken it, I would have.'

'But you never had the balls.'

'I had the balls. And the brains, son. The brains. The one thing you've managed to fry so completely with all your fucking drugs, might as well not have had any in the first place.'

Tony steps forward, inches from Dunc. Baring his teeth. An animal angered, but afraid to really strike out, just in case his prey really is stronger than it looks.

I see it for a second, beneath the bravado: the fear. Tony's still a wee kid at heart. Scared of his own shadow. Terrified of the consequences of talking back to his elders. And yet old enough to know how to hide that fear behind aggression.

He steps back, looks at me as though he's seeing me for the first time.

160

'The bollocks betrayed me,' he says. 'Betrayed us. You and me and Kat, we're all that's left now.'

I nod.

'You and me and Kat.' Repeating himself.

I want to tell him that it's just him. That's all now. I'm in this for one reason only: to save Kat. When I've done that, Tony can get whatever's coming.

'Time to clean house,' Tony says, decisive. 'Make a fresh start. Show this city we're not a joke.'

'Aye?'

'That prick Buchan's the key, man. We go play him along for a while...'

'And then take the power for yourself?' Dunc says.

'Way you laid it out, man. Before you got scared.'

'Before I got sensible.'

Tony laughs. Looks at me. Looks at the gun I'm holding. I figure he's going to ask for it back. But he doesn't. He grins. 'Can't trust anyone, man. I mean it – absolutely no-one. Everyone's got their own agenda. Even family. Even a retard like my brother, you can't trust him either. You know that, aye? That he's a retard? Why he's so good at killing. Doesn't understand pain, man. Doesn't feel it. Bloody eejit. Dad told me it wasn't a weakness, it was a strength. Always thought he was talking bollocks about that.' Tony thinks because Ray never speaks that he's slow as well as quiet. It's not true. Tonight's proof of that. Ray had a plan all along. Improvised, sure, but a plan. A goal.

Tony thinks of himself as a predator. He doesn't know shite. He's as delusional as me. All Tony is, is a messed up piñata of pure rage. Hang him up, hit him with a bat and all that will spill out is hate and horror and undeserved grudges.

Ray's the real shark. Hunts with purpose. Kills with reason.

'What I'm saying,' Tony says, 'is that I don't know I can trust even you any more, man. If this fat prick can betray my dad and then me within the space of a few days, and if my own brother can

161

try and kill me, then, you know, I gotta have some idea that I can trust you.'

He steps forward. His hands wrap around mine. And the gun.

'You won't do the powder with me no more, man. So you have to do something else. Aye?'

I have difficulty swallowing. Throat's closing up. Breathing feels shallow. Head's filling up with beer bubbles.

'I gave you the gun, man. I need you to show me you're not afraid to kill my enemies.'

'I'm not –'

'You've killed people, John. Thought you did anyway, didn't matter that the arsehole came back from the dead. There's no real difference now. Except you can see what you're doing. You can watch him die. There's no feeling like it, buddy. Nothing comes close. Drugs, sex, whatever.'

I look at Dunc. If I was in his place, I'd be making a break for it, trying to get out while the two fuckwits in the room had this stand-off about whether or not to end my life. But like I say, Dunc isn't afraid of death any more. What he is, he's accepting.

And somehow that's worse than if he was trying to run, trying to save his own skin.

'Do it, man,' Tony says. *Sotto* voice, now. Making a scene out of all this. Playing it for Dunc's benefit. 'Show me you have the balls.' Still with his hand on mine, maybe worried that I'll turn the gun on him. Restraining me, making sure I know that he's still got the power.

I need Tony alive and on my side. For now. He's my bargaining chip with Ray. The one thing I have that will pull the monster back out into the light. And this time, I'm not going to hesitate. I can't afford to.

I have to think of Kat.

I've been losing myself. Drowning in my cover, losing sight of who I am. I'd figured when I signed up to the operation, that it would help find who I really was. Instead I'm more fractured than before I began.

Time to reassert myself. Make a choice. Pull myself back together. Even if I'm not the same person I once was when it's done.

I have to be somebody.

'Do it,' Tony whispers.

I look at Dunc. His eyes meet mine. Looking older than they ever have before. Near completely black. I think of a wise old owl in a children's book. Someone who has the wisdom of the ages, who has nothing left to discover, who has accepted their life for good or ill. Earlier, I'd seen a scared old man, someone trying to desperately to save his own skin.

And now?

He nods. Maybe even smiles a little.

Tony steps back.

I'm still holding the gun. I take a deep breath.

Who am I? How far am I willing to go?

Time to find out.

I raise the gun. Fat Dunc, the traitor, the turncoat, the clapped out old bastard, closes his eyes.

I pull the trigger. And nothing happens.

Again.

Again.

Again.

Tony giggles, high-pitched and hysterical. He claps a hand on my shoulder. 'Should see your face, man! See your face!'

He whirls round, holds out one hand and shows me the clip from the gun. Laughs again. 'Nah, man, you ain't ready, not yet. Nice to know whose side you're on, though.' He presses the clip into my free hand. Then moves directly in front of Dunc, leans down and places his hands on the man's shoulders. 'You shite your breeks, old man? You scared?'

Dunc doesn't say anything.

Tony starts to massage the other man's shoulders. His hands

163

rolling the fat beneath them. 'Always liked you,' he says. 'Uncle Dunc. What we used to call you, growing up. Uncle Dunc. You were blood. Family.' His long fingers slip around Dunc's neck. 'Not any more.' He squeezes. Dunc doesn't react at first. Then he starts to gag, but doesn't fight back. His legs starts to kick up and down. He trembles all over. His skin starts to turn purple. His eyes bug. Tony increases the pressure, leaning down and into the other man, getting up close and personal, all the time watching as the panic increases in the old man's eyes.

But still Dunc doesn't fight back. His legs kick through instinct more than anything, and he gasps as his lungs struggle to figure out why he's just letting this psycho fuck choke the life out of him.

'Traitor! Turncoat! Fucking die!' That last word, a long, high-pitched howl of hatred as he puts his full weight around Dunc's neck and presses his thumbs against the other man's trachea.

Dunc goes limp. Tony continues to apply the pressure. Then, when he realises that Dunc is dead, he stands up and wipes his hands on the side of his shirt.

'Not family,' he says. 'Not any more.' He spits at Dunc's face. 'Now you're just a fat fucking corpse.'

Five

By All Means

2333 – 0234

Kat

Three years ago, a cop came to see me.

Suit and tie. Salt and pepper hair. No expression. Not once in our whole conversation. I wondered if that was for my benefit, or if his wife had to put up with that too.

He was married. Wore the ring in plain view. Sometimes he'd twist it about on his finger. Not that he wanted to take it off. More like he needed to fiddle with something. I figured when if he ever worked behind a desk, he'd be the kind to eat pens when he was thinking about a difficult problem. Maybe an ex-smoker, or maybe just too full of energy to ever really be still.

It wasn't my first visit from the polis, my family being the way they are. Even though they never had anything on me, every so often they'd come in, remind me who I was. As though they thought I'd just blurt out all the skeletons in our collective closet.

I never did.

Even when I wanted to.

Maybe now I regret that.

The detective's name was Crawford. He sat down on the sofa without asking permission. Entitlement, or maybe a psychological thing. He just sat, and waited for me to take the armchair opposite.

Only spoke when I sat down. Didn't make me think he had any power. Just got on my wick.

'Ms Scobie,' he said, and what I heard was all the old playground chant of *Scabies Scobie* and the phantom taste of the dirt that fat Jenny used to make me eat before Ray persuaded her that was a bad idea. Not his intention, but the mind can be strange that way. 'I want to show you something.'

He had a folder with him. Opened it on the coffee table. Made me lean forward to look. Made me wish I hadn't.

Men with their faces battered. Flesh raw purple and blue. Sightless eyes rolled back in sockets. Flesh mutilated with scars. Blood dried black. The kind of images ordinary, decent people think exists only on a bad episode of CSI, has no place on their doorsteps.

I swallowed back the nausea.

'Who were they?'

The copper – Crawford – rattled off names. Fast and easy. Maintaining eye contact the whole time, making his point clear. Each name was supposed to have impact, to show me something about Crawford and how he felt about my family, the way they impacted on other people's lives.

'You know what your family does. Who they are. Where the money comes from. Even if you never talk about it.' He looked around as though seeing the living room for the first time. 'This flat is owned by your uncle. You get a nice little discount, because what uncle wouldn't do a wee favour for his favourite niece?' The way he looked at the room, it was as though he was cataloguing how many lives this place cost.

When he spoke, he didn't vary his tone. Every word flat and even. Made me think of an older Keanu Reeves with a slight Island lilt replacing the California dude twang. 'These men paid for this place with their lives.' He paused. Not a hesitation. Giving me a moment to think. 'Your uncle says he's a self-made man. Fought his way out of poverty. Made something of himself. True enough, as far as these things go. And maybe things were different when he was young. But he never cared about any of that. Once he started hurting people, he couldn't stop. I think he enjoys it. And don't start me on your cousins.'

'Vicious rumours,' I said. 'Don't think I haven't heard –'

'Your uncle is a violent bastard. A man with an aptitude for hurting other people. When I joined the force, I worked with a Detective Inspector who told me that men of violence become one of two things. Cops or criminals. Depending on their conscience, on how they empathise with other people. The code your uncle instilled in the family, it wasn't about love. It was about protecting himself no matter what.'

'Detective...'

'Or maybe you'd like to talk about your cousins. Tony, the nutjob, or maybe Ray... Ray the killer. I mean, Jesus, you have to know...'

'That he's bad news? Aye, who doesn't? But –'

'But nothing! You can't live in denial, Kathryn.'

No-one calls me Kathryn. I'm Kat. Always Kat. Only my mother called me Kathryn. Only her.

'You can't live in denial,' Crawford said. 'Your family are bad news, always have been. You and your mother lived on the fringes. But you can't bury your head in the sand. One day you're going to need help. From someone like me. And there's going to be no-one around if they don't think you can be trusted.'

'I don't know anything.'

'You could if you wanted to.'

I knew what he was asking me. Maybe I should have done it. There was a part of me that knew what he was asking me was the right thing to do. It wasn't that I was scared. Not in the way he might have thought.

'What if I ask you to leave now?'

He didn't stand immediately, presented his hands to me, palm up. 'Then I'll leave. Never bother you again. But you have to know that I didn't come in here blind. We have good intelligence. I know who you are. Everything about you. I like to think I might know what kind of person you are too.'

'Yeah?'

'I know you have a degree you never used. You could have left Glasgow – your family – a long time ago but you never did. Maybe because of your mother's death, maybe because the big world seems too damn big. Maybe. Maybe. Maybe.'

'See, you don't know me.'

'You're clean, Kathryn. A citizen. The kind of person that I'm entrusted to protect. The kind of person who knows bad people when they meet then. The kind of person who has a conscience. But your family...'

I wanted to throw him out of the house, but I couldn't. Politeness, maybe. Coppers were the enemy, but I was the one who had invited him into my house. It would be wrong to shout and scream and throw him out for doing his job.

I'd always known Uncle Derek had dark secrets. That if I just got the courage to look, I'd be able to see them laid bare. But every time I worked up to it, I just had to turn away again, knowing that once I saw the truth I'd never be able to deny it.

This detective was asking me to look places I was scared to go.

And I couldn't. Not then. Maybe not ever. Not without being force to confront what I already knew.

'I want you to leave,' I said, polite as possible. 'Please, just get out.'

'I mean it,' Crawford said, finally standing up. 'I won't come back. I'll honour your request.'

'That's fine. That's great. Hunky dory.' I didn't intend sarcasm or passive aggressiveness. It just came out that way, and I felt a little kick of shame in my stomach.

'One day,' he said, 'you won't be able to ignore the truth any more. Won't be able to write Anthony off as just a wild lad. You'll be forced to think about his brother's silence. Realise that if he ever spoke about what he did, he'd be admitting to the worst kind of crimes. Jesus, you have to know what he did all those years ago. Right? Your ex-boyfriend?'

Maybe I gave something away then. I was trying my best not to react, but some things just hit you.

I kept my mouth shut. One thing about being a Scobie, you know it's best never to mouth off at the law even if you haven't done anything wrong.

The police aren't your friends. No matter what they tell you at school, what you see on the telly, what you read in books. The cops are the enemy. They're out to get you. Worse than the monsters who live in the cupboard or under the bed.

Mum used to laugh about when I was five years old and the police came to my school to give a road safety talk. They'd come in with some guy in a massive rodent outfit. Safety Squirrel, some shit like that. I'd been fine with the six-foot rodent. But when the cops entered the room, I'd jumped to my feet and yelled, 'Piiiigs!' at the top of my lungs.

'I don't know where she got it from,' Mum used to say and all her friends would laugh. But there was always something knowing in the laughter, some unspoken knowledge that had to be laughed away before anyone got too uncomfortable about it.

Mum was no crook. But she was a Scobie. By blood. So was I. Enough for certain things to hold true in my life.

When I let Crawford out, he stopped just before I had the chance to close the door on him. He looked at me with his big grey eyes. They were slightly out of proportion, I noticed, giving him a childlike appearance even though he was in his mid-forties. But when I thought he was about to say something, he suddenly turned away again. And walked.

I waited until he was out of sight before I closed the door again. Slowly. Quietly.

• • •

'Kat?'

I open my eyes.

It's cold.

I'm leaning against rough stone. My legs are stretched out in front of me.

The wind massages my face gently.

I look around. Make out shapes in the darkness. Headstones. Statues of angels standing guard over the dead.

Ray stands a little away from me. Looking down. I see the gun in his hands. He's shaking. You'd only notice you knew what you were looking for.

I wonder if he realises he's dying.

It's too late for him. It has to be. Maybe too late for both of us.

God only knows how strong the hate is that keeps him standing. So what's keeping me alive?

'Kat?'

'Aye?'

'I would have…saved your life.'

'I know.'

John

I'm out of the bathroom, wiping my hand across the back of my mouth. When I swallow, I taste the acidity of my own vomit.

I take deep breaths. Force it back.

Find my equilibrium.

In the mirror, I see something mocking in the face of the man who looks back at me. Like he knows all of this could have been avoided. Like he's watching some black comedy, can't believe just how dumb I've been to get into this mess in the first place.

Leaning against the wall, Tony points two fingers my way with his thumb cocked. Makes a motion like he's just fired off a shot, says, 'How you doing, killer?' Giggles. I figure he's done another line while my stomach was escaping through my mouth.

I ignore him best I can.

This is it, then. The step over the line. No going back. No more lying. I've made my choice. Decided once and for all who I am.

Tony comes over, puts his hands on my shoulders, looks me in the eye and says, 'Who's my number-one guy?' He cracks up after that.

Laughing at your own jokes. The true sign of a psychopath.

My phone goes off. I don't recognise the number.

'You going to answer that?'

I answer. Uncertain. It's a mobile number. Pretty sure it's not a PPI or marketing call. Of course, you never can tell.

A voice, rasping and broken, says, 'Put my...brother on.'

I don't know what to do. Just stand there, phone pressed to my ear, not moving, not saying a word.

'Hear me? Do it.' Then, as an afterthought: 'She's...alive. If you're... interested.'

I pass the phone to Tony. He doesn't understand, but takes it anyway. Turns his back on me, making it clear he doesn't want me in the same room.

'Aye?' He talks soft, like he thinks he might be able to stop me overhearing. 'Aye, it's finished, Ray. You're fucking finished.'

He doesn't say much else. Just listens. For a long time. Then hands back the phone, says, 'End game, then. Tonight. He dies.'

'And Kat?'

'I were you, I'd prepare for the worst.'

'He told me she was alive.'

'And you believe him?'

I almost say, *much as I believe any Scobie*. But catch the words before they leave my lips. Tony reads something into my silence. Says, 'Thought as much.' Then grins, shows off sharp incisors. 'Night's young yet.'

• • •

In the car he says, 'Family's everything to us. Know why?'

'Because of everything your dad fought for?' It wasn't a tough narrative. They talked about it so often that it was a wonder no-one else in the world knew the Edited Edition of the Great Scobie Family History.

'Family's all you have in the end. Lesson learned a long time ago. Our great-great-great-grandfather, he owned a factory. You believe that? We had money coming out our arses. Shat fucking gold bricks. To be a Scobie was to be fucking king of the world.'

He speaks with an edge of fanaticism, words running together, pitch rising. There's a glee in retelling the story, a complete belief in what he's saying. There's more than just drugs pumping through his system. More, even, than his own pumped-up ego. This is something inherited. Something fundamental. I imagine he'd been told the story over and over since he was a wee lad.

'And then we lost it all. The factories got fucked. The money vanished. The family lost everything, you know? All we had left was each other. That was what kept us going. By the time Dad was born we were living in this bloody run-down shithole in the Gorbals, with the Russians and the Jews, three kids to one room, that kind of crap. You hear people talk about how times were better despite the hardships, but the truth is, people just remember what they want. Dad's recollection is how much he hated this life he was born into, how he knew people had more than he did, how he fucking wanted it all.'

We're in the Clyde Tunnel now. Warning signs on the walls tell us that in the event of an emergency we have to leave our car behind and walk.

The strip lights overhead cast a strange hue, unusually harsh in stark contrast to the inky blue darkness out either side of the tunnel. I watch the walls flicker past. Tony either doesn't notice I'm somewhere else or didn't care. When he talks, he just expects that you're listening.

'So he took it. The only way he could. Did it all for his family. His fucking family, you understand that? That's what it was like for him. And I always got it, you know? What the old man went through, what he had to do to get all of that. I fucking admire him for it.'

And yet, I think, you killed him. Or at least, you were responsible for his death. You planned to betray him.

'He lived too long, maybe. But you have to admire his balls, doing what he did. And I don't think everyone understands that.

My aunt never did, Kat's mum. She was born later, ten fucking years later, kind of an accident, but still, she was loved. My dad, after their parents died, he raised her himself. And she had the nerve to turn her back on what he did, call him a criminal to his face. And worse. I saw it once, you know, when she'd got shitfaced on wine. She screamed at him in front of his sons, told him that he was fucking evil, that she should turn him in.' He shakes his head at the memory.

We're out of the tunnel now, heading towards the centre of town. On either side of the dual carriageway, the buildings flick past in a stream of lights.

I'm tired. My head pounds from the inside, like my brain's swelling up, desperate to escape the confines of my skull. All I want is to sleep for a little while. The day's been long. My life is long. The weight of everything I've done, all the secrets I've kept, is finally too much for me to keep in the air.

'I wanted to kill her. I fucking did. I was ten years old, but I would have throttled her, same as I did with that fat fuck tonight. But the old man, he knew what I'd seen, and he pulled me aside, told me that she was family, that she didn't really understand, but she was still family, and it was our duty to protect her. Family is everything, he said. Blood really is thicker than water. That was why he'd done everything he'd done. Become someone that certain people would hate. All for his family. No regrets about that, he said. No fucking regrets. In this world, people can only look out for their own.'

And yet you planned to betray him. And you tried to murder your own brother.

He's talking now with a distracted air, divided between memories and concentrating on the road ahead. 'Both me and Ray understood what he was saying. But I guess I'm the one with the brains, because there's times when you can't let sentiment get in the way of what you do, know what I'm saying?'

'You think your dad should have killed your aunt?'

'Maybe. Don't know that she ever did go to the coppers, like. But you never know.'

There's silence for a moment. I don't have the energy to figure the contradictions in Tony's life or inside his head. He's just a bastard psycho. Believes what he says, jumps through hoops to justify his own hypocrisy. In his head, he is as justified as his father. Maybe more so. He's a product of his the society he grew up: the perfect image of the self-centred '80s Greed is Good philosophy. He wanted it all, but unlike his father, his motivations were always self-centred. If it feels good, do it. He can't think about anyone beyond himself. It's what stops him from ever forming any kind of human connection, makes him turn to drugs for any sense of reality in the world.

His talk of family, it's all lip service.

Makes me think of my father. A man who talked about God and forgiveness, then beat the shite out of the Catholic lads on a Friday night after downing enough pints to dull the pain of them punching back.

'Ray heard the same speeches,' Tony says. 'Think he still believes all the shite my father spun.'

'Aye?'

'Why else would he choose to end it tonight? Out there of all places too.'

'Out where?' He still hasn't told me what Ray said on the phone, where we're going once we meet Pete and Al.

'The Necropolis,' he says. 'The old family plot. Christ. Maybe he's gone poetic. High off the blood loss. Retard. Like it matters. It's right enough he should die there. A dead man among the fucking dead men.' He laughs.

The weight I feel gets worse. Threatens to crush me completely.

Kat

It's cold.

The sky is an inky shade of blue, and there's a surprising amount of light once your eyes get used to it.

I'm trying not to think about Lesley. All she did to get killed was what she had been told to do all her life – call the police. *They will come and save you.* Except they didn't.

And her friends?

Well, I let her die. Make of that what you will.

Time and again, my cousins have got away with all the things you're supposed to be banged up for: dealing drugs, laundering cash, hurting people, even murdering them.

I forgave them every time. Why? Because I grew up believing that's what family was all about. You stick by your own. No matter what. You forgive them the greatest sins. Just because you're supposed to.

I always wondered where we got that from. Why my mother bought into it. Because it was her brother pulled the family out of the slums? Because she really believed it? Or because she was indoctrinated as much as anyone?

Family.

I say, 'Do you enjoy it?'

He's leaning against the crypt walls. This small house that celebrates what used to be our family. Back before we were thrown into poverty, forced to reinvent ourselves. This tomb is all that's left.

Doesn't even really belong to the family any more. No-one cares for it. The weather and the harsh nights have eroded the stonework, turned the monument to a shabby shadow that hides from the world. The angel who sits on top of the roof has his wings clipped. Half his face has eroded, become a featureless lump of granite that only hints at past majesty. Looking at it in the half-light, I think of Ray. Both of them eroding. Slowly. Piece by piece. And like Ray, the angel doesn't even notice. No pain. No sensation.

I keep drifting. Into my own thoughts. Slipping deep into my mind, forgetting the world around me. My middle is cold now. My stomach feels like it's pumped full of the freezing anaesthetic that the dentist uses.

The wind is sharp, though. Keeps me conscious. Cuts through my blouse. Scratches the skin beneath like ragged fingernails. I wrap my arms around me. A futile effort to keep warm. I wonder if it's the night air or the shock. Am I too far gone for it to matter?

Ray says, 'Came here…with Dad. When we…were kids. Told us this is…what we used to be. His dad…brought him too.' He takes a deep breath. Even speaking is becoming difficult for him. His lungs aren't filling up properly. It's not just the burning of his throat affecting his speech. I wonder if he knows what's happening inside him.

'Family's everything…he said.'

'You killed him.'

'He…started it.' Sounding petulant. Childish. Makes me want to laugh. But I suppress the giggle trying to fight its way out of my chest.

Just that effort hurts. A lot. Pins and needles shoot through my whole body. How long have I got left?

He had been prepared to save me. Take me to the hospital. Sacrificing his own need for revenge, ending this night of violence, to save me. And I stopped him.

Why?

My feet are wet. My shoes aren't designed for this weather, for hanging around graveyards at night. The liquid soaks through my socks. I wiggle my toes, for all the good it does. Remember when I was a kid how when I got cold at night, I'd massage the duvet with my feet for warmth. And comfort too.

I look around. At the headstones, markers and tombs. Think

of the grandeur that this was place was designed to convey, how death was something to be proud of. How these people prepared for their deaths. How much things have changed. How we have lost respect for death.

When I was a student, I shared a flat with a girl called Amy. The kind of girl guys turned their heads to look at. And she didn't even try. Had this whole Goth thing going on, dyed her blonde hair black, covered herself up, and still remained desirable to guys.

She called me one night, asked if I could pick her up from the police station. I remember asking her what happened. She said she didn't want to talk on the phone. Only told me after half a bottle of wine back at the flat that she'd been caught in the Necropolis with a boy she'd picked up at a club. How she had this thing for graveyards. 'Fucking among the dead,' she said, shaking her head. 'Nothing like it for feeling alive.'

Can't say I ever tried it. Wonder if I should have. Wonder if I should have done a lot of things.

Ray's makeshift bandages, torn from his jacket and jersey, aren't working. The blood's seeping out of me.

I'm too cold. Definitely more than just the night air.

My brain's slowing down too. I can barely concentrate on any one thought at a time. Jumping in and out memory and the here and now. I concentrate on the present. Just need to keep my brain here, keep it focused on the real world.

'What now?' I ask Ray. Just to do something. Keep myself from drifting too far.

'We wait,' he says. Shaking. Shivering. He may not feel much, but his body still reacts when it has no other choice.

I close my eyes. Just for a moment. One moment. A little rest. Get this picture of Lesley's face, eyes open wide, lips dropped as though to say something, colour drained from around her cheeks. Eyes are a little wet, like she's ready to start crying. But she doesn't get the chance. Because he shoots her. No warning. No final chance. No mercy. No joy, even.

I might have been able to understand if he was the kind of stone-cold who took pleasure in hurting people. But he's emotionless. Pragmatic. I've seen it more times that I care throughout this one evening.

Ray checks his gun. He's been doing this every few minutes. A habit? Ensuring that he's prepared? Checking the chamber, the clip, slamming it home into the grip.

I watch him do all this. Disconnected and powerless. Like I'm not really here.

I never hurt anyone in my life. Not intentionally. Never raised my fists in anger. Never took a weapon with the intention of using it against someone. Of course I've raised my voice and said things designed to hurt, but no more than normal people do. I'm no saint, would never claim to be. But I'm no killer either.

I'm a Scobie. Except I'm not.

At least that's what I've always thought.

Like that Detective, Crawford, said, I'm a citizen. Don't break any laws. Don't hurt people. Just live my life. Work in a hospital. Make up for everything that my cousins, my uncle, all their bloody cronies, have ever done. Is that enough? Or am I as complicit in their bad deeds as anyone?

That's what Crawford thought. I could see it in the way he looked at me, that he was selling me a line, but he thought I was every bit as bad as Uncle Derek, Tony and Ray. Not because of what I had done. Because of what I never did.

I could blame the code. I grew up with it. Understood it as a fact of life. How can you just turn your back on something like that?

Never grass.

Never tell.

Never betray.

'Kill me,' I say, and the wind catches my words. I try not to think about what happened the last time I asked him.

Ray looks at me. His brow knots, eyebrows floating closer

together. 'What?'

I can't take it back. 'If you're going to kill them, kill me too.' I'm dying anyway. Can feel it. That bullet's inside me. I'm cold. Shivering. Just want it over. To close my eyes and go to sleep. Never wake up.

He shakes his head.

'You can't feel pain,' I say.

He shakes his head.

Can I make him understand? 'Can you feel anything?'

He squats beside me. His eyes are wide. There's a curiosity there, and I recognise a childlike quality. For all that he's done, for all that he's seen, I think maybe he still views the world with wonder. Not really understanding it, but desperate to know things in the way that other people do.

Our faces are maybe an inch apart. His breath is warm. I can hear his lungs fill and expand. The sound is watery, clogged. We're close. Very close.

'Not pain,' I say. 'But you have to feel other things. I mean, pleasure?'

His breathing escalates.

Something in the back of my mind clicks. A moment of revelation.

He killed my boyfriend for cheating on me. I always tried to believe it was someone else, or that it was an accident, but I've always known the truth. Ray killed for me.

His breath is shallow. If I concentrate, I can feel the pulse of his heart beating in his chest.

Less than an inch apart.

My right hand comes up, brushes his cheek. He's breathing so hard, he might pass out.

I scratch at his face. Hard. Nails rip into skin. Blood trickles between my fingers. I pull down slowly, painfully, agonisingly.

He doesn't flinch.

I pull back.

He stays hunkered down, still one hand holding the gun, the other rising to touch where I scratched him. When he pulls it away, he looks at his hand, and his brow furrows. Like he can't understand why he's seeing blood.

I say again, 'Kill me. If you're going to kill everyone else, you might as well kill me.'

Scorched earth. Isn't that what they call it? When you burn everything. Leave nothing behind. At heart, I'm a Scobie. As corrupt as the rest of them. Even if just through inaction.

'Aye,' he says. 'I will.'

I think of all the people who died before and after I threw Crawford out of my house, refused to help him in his cause. All the people in thrall to my uncle, my cousin Tony, the drug addicts and degenerates. The gamblers taken in, all the weak, weak men lured by the promise a cheap encounter in a sauna that always cost them more than they'd ever expect.

I was guilty by omission. Complicit. Deliberately dumb and blind. I'd known the truth all the time. Just never admitted it because the idea was too terrifying to admit.

Ray gets to his feet. Looks at me for a moment. Still holding the gun.

The clip is full. He's ready for the oncoming storm. Can he waste one bullet?

I hold my breath.

Unable to read the expression on his face.

John

'We tried twice before.' Crawford told me. 'Inserting people into the network, working them up the chain.'

'What happened?'

Crawford spun the folder across the table. Printouts fanned over the faux wood surface. Hi-res, art-framed, but brutal. Men disfigured and dead. Tortured. Brutalised. The kind of things you saw in flashes on the TV, but momentary and blurred. In real life, you couldn't look away, couldn't cut to the next scene.

'Your predecessors.'

My predecessors.

'You know this isn't the way to keep me interested in the job?'

Except it was. He knew it. Could see in my eyes that I wasn't worried about dying. Could read in my file that I had no family, no real friends, no connections.

It wasn't simply that I was unafraid of death. Just that it wouldn't have too many repercussions.

There was silence between us.

The men on the table with their eyes still open stared at us.

'What happened to blow their cover?'

'The Scobie boys aren't daft. Not even Tony.' Aye, well, it's easy to underestimate a psychopath.

Of the three, Tony was the most unstable. I'd seen lots of paper on him. Most of it should never have crossed my eyes, but there and ways and means of seeing things you're not supposed to. Crawford knew that, and I guess it was one of the reasons he'd brought me on board. I was adaptable. Didn't care so much about following procedure as doing what needed to be done.

Even back when I came in, word was floating around about the SCDEA's future. The joint operation that Crawford had set up was in danger of becoming obsolete. Time was a factor. There could be no more mistakes. No more dead men.

I was the man Crawford was willing to put his faith in. What did that say about his judgement of character?

Back then, I was the kind of arsehole he wanted undercover. The kind of man who might be able to form a bond with Tony Scobie. On paper, I was a pretty shitty copper, but I could make a great wannabe criminal.

What I read about Anthony Scobie told me that he was a narcissistic personality type, prone to violent outbursts, and lacking in impulse control. He was of high intelligence, maybe higher than most. But he was unable to focus that intelligence, make it mean anything. He remained in his father's shadow. Never stepped up. Never took charge of anything. But he always talked about it, told people that one day he'd be running things.

So why didn't he just reach out and take what he wanted? Because he didn't really want to? Or because Dad refused to grant him any kind of power and despite all his talk, Tony was really scared of the old man?

It was hard to say. Even after a year and a half undercover, I can't give you a clear answer.

I said to Crawford, 'Tell me how they blew their cover.'

'We don't know. We just… We have to try and feed you into the food chain from a new angle. They won't trust anyone coming in on outside reference. Or even inside, now. Derek Scobie's paranoia's got him close to breaking point. One of these poor bastards, we put him in a cell next to one of Tony's goons. He had no ties back to the force. Nothing on paper. Nothing to say who he was. He got close… Closer than anyone else.'

'And then he got dead.'

'Aye, that's it.'

I thought about the pictures.

'How do I approach this?'

'Social angle, that's what we figure. Get close to the family, make it clear you're up for sale, maybe, that you're someone they can use.'

'A dirty copper?'

'No. It's too close… Too much risk.'

'Then what?'

'You joined the force after university, right? You were going to be an accountant?'

'Right. My dad thought it would be respectable.'

'We use that. The Scobies run a lot of business through fronts. Ones they own directly, others they swallow up when things go bad for the owners.'

'They need people to cook the books.'

'Exactly.'

'It's been a long time since uni. I can barely remember how to spell accountancy… Besides, I only just scraped a pass. I wasn't interested in –'

'That's even better.'

'Aye?'

'If you were good at your job, why would they need you? Gives them something to lean on you with. Try and convince you're not where you should be. You deserve better. They know if you were that good, they wouldn't be able to touch you. They need a loser, someone they can boss around. Let them see that. Let them make the offer first.'

'They don't have their own people?'

'Arrangements can be made. Derek and his boys may keep themselves clean, but the people beneath them…we can make life tough.'

'Bit of a coincidence if I just turn up.'

'Life is full of them. Have you ever thought about that?' Crawford leaned across the table.

He had a point. Coincidence was a part of life. Coincidence had brought us together. So why was my stomach churning? It wouldn't be my first time undercover. I'd worked stings before: short-term operations with quick pay-offs. But this would be an extended gig.

With one difference.

We had no time to set up properly. We had to play it by ear. Drop me in at the deep end. With the SCDEA's time running out, and pressure coming from above regarding the operation, Crawford wanted me in fast.

'You really think I'm the man for the job?'

'Yes.'

'Burke doesn't.' Putting it mildly. First time I was called in to discuss the operation, Burke had been in the room. He was Crawford's number two, saw it as his job to play devil's advocate, shooting down everything he could, making sure no-one was cutting corners, no-one was taking the job less than seriously. And I guess he'd figured the best way to do that was to get in my face, pick my faults, tell me I was fucked before I even started.

Tough love? The toughest.

'In his own way, he does.'

'Prick has a funny way of showing it.'

'You should see how he was with the other candidates.'

'Any reason?'

'Just his way.'

'When do I start?'

'You're sure?'

I'd been sure since they first told me what this was about. Since they first mentioned the name *Scobie*.

This was my shot at the big time. The chance to really contribute. To find out what I was made of.

Was I worried?

I thought about the images again. They worried me. Knowing how those poor bastards died. In pain. Alone. But then, I'd always been alone. Made sense for me to die that way, if I had to.

Maybe that's the way Crawford saw it too, even if he wasn't being direct.

'I'm sure.'

• • •

In the passenger's seat, thinking about how I got here.

We pull over, park in the shadow of the bridge on Wishart Street. The street is empty. There's something strange about the emptiness, a quiet and stillness I don't usually associate with Glasgow. Maybe it's the dead that sleep on either side of the road.

In the near distance, the high lights of office buildings spark in the skyline beyond the edge of the Cathedral that sits proud in the moonlight.

Tony, in the driver's seat, says, 'She'll be fine, man.' I don't say anything. 'You still love her? I mean, despite everything that happened?'

'Aye, I do.'

And that was maybe the only true thing about me. I was a fake as a cop. Fake as a criminal. I didn't know who I was, what I wanted.

The one thing I should have been faking was the only thing that was true.

Tony was quiet for a moment. 'Then she'll be fine.'

Platitudes. I think he's reassuring himself as much as me. Can't figure why Tony's so attached to her, but he is. Sometimes he says that he owes her his life, but won't tell me why. Maybe its hyperbole. Doesn't matter. It's useful to me here and now. Means I can use him to bargain for her life.

If she's still alive.

Dunc told me she was shot. The way the world works is that men like Ray keep going, while the innocent suffer.

But I have to try.

I say, 'She made me feel like I wasn't alone.' My cheeks burn. I don't know why I spoke, exposing myself to him like that. I look out of the passenger window at the slopes of the Necropolis across the road.

'That's love,' Tony says, and for a second I think he means it. Then, changing the subject, and his tone, fast: 'Well, at least my brother wasn't lying.'

186

On the other side of the road, on the other side of the bridge, there's another car. I recognise it. Same model of Megane I saw Kat driving after the wake. Only a few hours ago, but I'm so tired it could have been days.

It would make sense to take things slow and cautious. But what I do is jump out the car and run towards the other vehicle. Press my face against the windows on the driver's. There are dark stains on the seats.

Blood?

Whose?

Is Kat really still alive?

'What the fuck're you doing, you eejit?' Tony's right behind me. Grabs me by the collar, spins me round and shoves me so that I slam against the body of the car. He's in my face. I can smell his breath, rancid, hot and rotting. 'Could be anything in there. The bastard could be waiting for us.'

We're both still for a moment. But nothing happens.

Tony keeps hold of me with one hand, uses the other to jab an index finger against my forehead. 'Think before you act.' He lets go, pushing me away from him again, walks into the middle of the road and spits. 'Pillock,' he mutters.

My breath catches. I force it out, get this sharp, cold sensation right beneath my breastbone as if the air in my lungs is turning to ice. I watch Tony stand completely still in the middle of the road. He looks at the ground, like he's trying to figure something out. But then there's the noise of a car approaching, and he steps back beside me.

The headlights come in from John Knox Street, to the south. We wait for them to reach us. The vehicle slows down and pulls in behind Ray's car.

Wayne and Pete climb out. They're packing, guns out. No chances being taken tonight. Blood has already been spilt. The fuck does it matter now if the police catch up to them? This is about something deeper than the law.

Tony says, 'You know the plan, then.'

Pete says, 'No worries.'

Wayne gives me a wink. The expression on his face makes me think of a little boy who's finally been around to ride with the firemen and set off the blue lights.

They both carry the Glocks with confidence, maybe living out some kind of fantasy in their own heads. Dressed in shellsuit bottoms and Adidas tops, they don't look as kick-arse as they might believe. They cross the road, jump the fence and climb the incline towards the Major Archibald Douglas Monteath Mausoleum. Keeping to the shadows. Hunched over.

I think about when I first met them, Pete telling me about Wayne's fantasies of being Jack Bauer from *24*. The kind of fantasies that tend to go wrong when brought into the real world.

Tony looks at me, says, 'Come on, then,' and starts to walk the direction that Pete and Wayne drive in from. Two minutes to the end of the road, we hop the locked gates and follow the main path into the Necropolis.

This time of night, the Necropolis takes on an odd power. The creeping shadows of the monuments to lives lived, the still of the night, the quiet that falls within its confines as though the noises of the living are too afraid to impose. An atmosphere that tickles somewhere at the base of the neck. As though there is something lurking in the shadows. Watching. Waiting.

There are things there. Moving in places they can't be seen. Drug addicts looking for shelter. Foxes and night time scavengers.

And, tonight, killers waiting for a reckoning.

We walk deeper into the city of the dead.

I look at my watch. Nearly 3am. The sun comes up at around half seven now. By the time it does, all of this will be over.

One way or another.

Kat

I'm looking at the stars. And I'm alive.

My back is cold, but not uncomfortable. Something about the way the damp seeps through my clothes makes me feel more awake that I've been in a long time. The solidity of the stone connects me to the world.

I'm alive.

I'm looking at the stars and I'm alive.

I should be dead. After everything that's happened, I should be dead.

I say, 'Thank you.' Not really sure who I'm speaking to. Surely not God. I gave up on Him before I even hit my teens, and we certainly haven't been on speaking terms since Mum's death. I still visit his house, drink his wine, but it's more habit than anything.

Ray is silent. He's on his feet, waiting patiently. If I turn my head, I can see his feet and just beyond them the case. He's completely still. Might as well be one of the statues dotted around here.

I say, again: 'Thank you.'

'You're talking to me?'

I smile. 'I don't see anyone else here.' Then I turn my head again to look at the stars. 'You killed a man because he hurt me.' My mind starts racing through my life. Remembering little moments here and there. Seeing on the news what Ray did to the boy who broke my heart. Holding Mum's hand and knowing she couldn't respond. Laughing with a boy whose name I can't even remember when we slid round the tin-can waltzers at the fair.

Disconnected moments. Memories of a life I wish I remembered better.

'I'd have gone back to him, you know. Because I was too young and too stupid to know better.'

'Who?'

For the first time since I saw the news, I say his name. 'Andy.'

'I never...said –'

'I knew. I knew you killed him. Maybe even why.'

He doesn't respond. I can't see, but I think he might be blushing.

'You killed Lesley.'

That kills the mood. He won't look at me.

'Not for you. She was…in my way. Warned her.'

'Because she tried to call the police?'

'Told her not to. Told her she…would be okay if…. she didn't do…anything stupid.'

'Most people wouldn't consider calling the police to be stupid.'

'Would you? Call them?'

'No.'

He takes that as his answer.

I try to make him understand. 'But I'm a Scobie.'

'Blood. Not nature.'

'What's that mean?'

He doesn't say anything.

Slowly, my muscles weak now, I pull my knees to chest and wrap my arms round them for warmth.

I sat like this on beaches when I was a child. Sitting in the sand for hours, staring out at the sea, watching the waves lap gently against each other. Excited by froth, by the idea that there was something violent just beneath the surface of the water. Always wanting to dive in, see the waves from underneath, experience the world from a whole new perspective.

Never did, though. Much as I loved to watch, I was always too scared to dive in. Never even took a dip in a swimming pool. I shower rather than bath.

Call it a quirk. Or, like Tony does, call it messed up. Which is rich, coming from him.

Ray says, 'Someone's coming.' He's alert, standing straight.

I push back against the stone. My side screams with agony as I move. But I need to be on my feet. I place the back of my hands against the tomb, walk myself upright. The tears come heavy, but I don't make a sound.

Two men come into view, walking the main path. I can tell who they are just by the dark outlines, the way they carry themselves.

Tony walks with a hard-man swagger. His legs are bowed, like a cowboy. He doesn't slow down, doesn't hesitate. Beside him, John. More hesitant, less certain.

John, my former fiancé. John, the man who betrayed me.

And my family.

My heart skips beats. More threatening than the kind of skips you get when you're in love. I think about a song my mum and dad used to sing, back when I was a kid. My heart does the same kind of rhythm they would sing about.

Not for the reasons you might think. The beating is urgent. Insistent. Hateful. I want to run to him and scream and punch and kick and spit. But all I can do is stand still.

No choice in the matter. If I even try, I'll collapse. Already, my legs are disconnected from the rest of my body. I want to float away from all of this. All that's keeping me here is the cold stone of the Scobie mausoleum and the damp creeping under my clothes, sparking sensations in my skin. Tiny shocks that keep me conscious.

Tony and John get close, but not too close.

Everyone keeping their distance. Tony showing that his hands are empty. John hanging back, still acting like he doesn't really know what's going on.

Just some guy, you know? Aye, right. What does he imagine will happen when I discover the truth?

A few years back, the papers exposed a cop after years of working undercover with environmental activists. Published story after story about how everyone who knew him was betrayed when his superiors finally pulled him from the operation. How could they not feel betrayed? They'd allowed him into their circle. Let him form relationships. Not just friendships or casual acquaintances: he'd allowed people to fall in love with him.

How had they felt? His lovers? How badly were they betrayed?

Maybe I was beginning to understand. Maybe that's what's keeping me on my feet. Same way that Ray kept standing because he felt his principles had been betrayed by his brother and his father, I was standing because of my hate for John.

There's part of me that's surprised to see John here. When I heard Ray tell Tony the truth, I figured he would turn up in some back alley with a bullet through the back of his skull. But he's here. Maybe twelve feet away from me. Why is he still alive? What lies did he tell to get himself off the hook?

I always said I was a pacifist, that violence was the last resort. Defended the fact that the UK abolished the death penalty, said that it was harder to forgive than it was to swear vengeance.

And yet I want to scream out how it's not fair that John's skull is intact, that no-one put a bullet in him.

It's a small part of me, but one I can't deny. Not any longer. It's in me, the violence. This evening has taught me that. Everything I've seen, I should be on the ground. Weeping. Sick to my stomach just thinking about my best friend with her face blown in.

But I'm not sick. Sad. But not sick. Sad because it was a waste. Sad because she was a good person.

But not sick about what happened to her. Not disgusted or terrified or appalled.

Tony speaks first: 'The fuck are you? Lazarus?'

Ray doesn't answer. Simply says, 'I didn't betray you.'

'I know.'

Ray shifts his weight. Facing them down. Looking at him, I can't stop thinking of gun fighters in the Western movies that my uncle loved so much. We used to spend Easter weekends with him watching Technicolor and Cinemascope gunfights taking place on back-lot deserts.

Is that what Ray sees in his mind, now? Is this High Noon at the OK Corral? Tie a bloodied ribbon round the dead oak tree?

'You're a stupid fuck, Ray!' Tony, kicking it up a gear. Frustrated because his brother doesn't get what's going on. 'You're my brother, but you're a stupid fuck. I was the one skimmed the cash, set up the hit to look like it was you. I'm the one went over to Buchan. The one with the bloody brains!'

'Why?'

'Why? You were the one protecting dad. The one everyone was afraid of. The old bastard was just a figurehead. Nothing. A shuffling corpse. A relic. Without you, he was nothing. Everyone knew it. But he had you, his big bad bastard monster. The one who could kill people without batting an eyelid.'

Ray doesn't say anything. Shifts his weight a little, like his legs are getting tired. Almost imperceptible, but if you're looking close you'll see it.

I wonder how long he has.

What Lesley threatened: internal bleeding. Organs filling up with blood. Everything inside messed up. Eventually, he's just going to collapse. Stop working.

For years, he's been his father's toy soldier. Wind him up, let him go. The man without pain. Without fear. Without anything.

'I mean it,' Tony says. 'I mean, how could you not realise? You were a mistake, Ray. Your mother, she died giving birth to you. Says something, doesn't it, that my mother took you in and raised her as her own? But we were a generous fucking family. You were this sick kid. But we took care of you. Remember Doc Rennie? The old soak he was, used to take payment in booze from Dad to come treat you.'

Ray says, 'I remember.'

'What else do you remember?'

'Was special.'

'Special?'

'Dad told me. Special. Like no-one else. Could do...things. Others won't. You...you're sick. Violent.'

'Me?'

'You...like to hurt. I...don't care.'

Tony says, 'Fuck you, then, you lump of bastard rock. And fuck memory lane. Didn't come here to talk about old times.'

Ray says, 'Thought you'd…have killed him.' Meaning John.

Tony says, 'Bullshit. He's no cop. The shite he's done, Ray. You know that he's the one set the bomb? Got fucking high with me, ran up lines, said let's kill the retard bastard.'

Again, there's that shifting weight. Am I the only one who notices? Can't be discomfort. Something else. I've seen that movement before. Realise what's going to happen.

I should let Ray do it. That's what I want, right? That's why we're here. I put myself at risk so Ray could have his revenge. So I could watch him kill his brother. So I could unleash his vengeance on the man who hurt me. Broke my heart.

Just a little history repeating. All I have to do is stand back and watch.

I know what's coming. Can see the way his body tenses.

I close my eyes. See Lesley's face. The way her own eyes widen as she realises what's happening, and then the way they go cold, suddenly, as she slips away from this world quickly and easily.

No, I've accepted death. Accepted who and what I am. A Scobie. Steeped in violence and death.

But is that really who I am? Who I want to be?

I push off the cold stone, stumble run forward and jump at Ray, grabbing his arm like it's a branch and I'm swinging myself up onto it. The unexpected weight throws him off and he stumbles.

My side burns. The wound rips. I can feel it gaping, the blood pouring out. My blouse sticks against my skin.

The gun goes off.

The pain is like lightning that lances through me. My ears pop. I can't hear anything. I close my eyes, hang onto Ray's arm and realise that I'm screaming but the sound is little more than a distant buzz, a bee trapped in a jam jar.

Ray shakes me off. I hit the ground hard, roll onto my back, and think that's it, I'm dead. When Ray's done with them he'll kill me.

If I'm not already gone.

I can't move. The pain is uncomfortably numb.

Someone yells, 'Fuck you, you prick!' Sounds like they're shouting from the wrong end of a megaphone.

I force my head up, look past Ray, and see two figures coming from the other side of the hill. Their silhouettes are unmistakeable. Pete and Wayne. Two of the kindest guys my cousins ever knew. Their arms are raised. I know they're holding guns.

They take aim. Fire. Continuously.

I should roll out of the line of fire, away from Ray, from the chaos. But I can't move. My body refuses to obey. It's too late.

Ray stays standing. His body jerks with each shot. Blood soaks through his clothes. He stands there and takes it all.

The gunfire stops. The silence seems louder than the noise.

Ray turns his head to look at me, and his lips move. The movement is creaky, like a doll in a horror movie that's coming to life.

His clothes are blood stained rags.

I taste something in the back of my throat. Coppery. Thick. Unpleasant. A phantom taste.

Ray steps forward. Falls to his knees. His body twists, goes back, slips to the side.

The silence roars. I lay my head back on the grass. Look at the stars. Someone's hands are on my shoulders. I turn my head and see John. Surprisingly, I'm not angry any more. Just empty.

He mouths something. There is no sound. No sense of the world around making any noise. Nor even the rustle of my clothes or the gentle noise of crushed grass that you can hear in the dead silence of the evening.

John lets go. Moves over to where the three other men are standing over the corpse of my cousin.

He pulls a gun from his waistband. As though suddenly remembering it's there.

He stands behind Tony as though to get a better view. Shoots him in the back of the head.

Pete and Wayne too.

The sound roars back. The rush is too much. I let myself fall again.

It's all I can do.

John

I don't feel anything.

Remorse. Pity. Anger. Fear. Satisfaction.

Nothing.

I'm empty. Detached.

Who am I? I'm a killer.

This is no moment of epiphany. This is where I've been heading to for a long time.

I turn away from the pile of bodies, walk to Kat. She's lying on the grass, eyes open, but she doesn't seem to be looking at anything in particular.

I kneel beside her, notice the dark stain around her stomach. I put my hands on her midriff, feel the thick, unmistakeable gloop of blood.

All this, and she's dying. Is this how it ends? No grand heroic rescue. No sweeping music. Just death.

I thought Ray was the killer. But maybe death follows me around. Maybe I'm the reason all these people had to die.

I say, 'I love you.'

She looks at me. Doesn't say anything.

'I...love you.' Saying it again feels awkward, unnatural, forcing a point that's already been dismissed.

She swallows, forcing the action, as though something's stuck in her throat. She turns her eyes away to look up at the skies, and laughs. It's a short, sharp sound. Bitter, almost. There's a little gurgle behind it, like she's halfway through swallowing a glass of water.

She says, 'How can I believe that?' Then: 'Who are you?'

Who am I? A cop? A killer? A liar? The devil himself? Or just a stupid man who made some bad decisions, got carried away in his own lies?

'I…I know you won't believe me…but…I would have told you. Everything.'

'Are you serious?'

'Yes.'

She closes her eyes. My hands remain pressed against her belly. The blood leaking from her wound is thick, the flow slowing.

Is she dying?

I think about when we used to lie in bed together. All the times we did nothing but look at each other, not searching for anything in the other's eyes, just losing ourselves.

'You lied to me…' I have to strain to hear her. '…who you were.'

'Yes.' I lied. About a lot of things.

'You're polis.' Louder, this time. Spitting out the word.

'Yes.' But, now, never again. I've killed men this evening. Tony called me *killer*, thinking he was being funny. But there was nothing funny about it.

She says, 'Fuck you.'

Might as well have slapped me.

I get lightheaded. My breath catches sharp, a metal shard in my lungs. This isn't what I wanted. I wanted to save her. I wanted to run away with her. Start again.

I say, 'Come with me.' Still deluding myself.

'I'd rather die.'

She means it. This isn't the blood loss, or stress or confusion. I wonder how long she's been hanging on, whether the only thing keeping her upright was getting to say those words to me.

I look up at the statue of an angel who perches the side of the Scobie tomb, an imposing figure with a hood covering its face and a sword in its hand. Its features have been stripped and smoothed by the elements. But it still looks at me with a strange sneer scarring its features.

I want to weep.

But I have to make a choice. Stay here too long, and it's all over. There's no beginning again, with or without Kat.

I have to make a decision.

I take one last look at Kat. Her eyes are closed. Her breathing's shallow.

I drop the gun.

She's not coming with me.

If I stay with her, then my own life is over.

She'll be fine.

She'll be fine.

I have only one choice left.

I run.

• • •

My whole life running.

From family. Life. Myself.

That's why I applied for the undercover assignment. Figured it would help sort me out, let me start again, resolve the mistakes I'd already made.

During the early stages, Burke and Crawford asked about my family. Probed and prodded. Burke told me how I would never be any good for undercover because my family was too rich, too middle class, too normal.

Precisely why I was perfect, you asked me. I hated my family. My life.

That was why I became a cop. Because then my father wouldn't speak to me. Or, at least, I wouldn't have to speak to him.

Passive aggressive. But still a kind of running.

In secondary school, there was this girl named Aileen. What I remember most about her was her hair. Long. Blonde. All the way down her back, the tips skating against her backside. She had the kind of smile that teenage boys lose all their sense over. And she loved me. In that full-on, teenage hormonal way. I knew it, felt the same way, much as I feared it.

The plan became this: we'd go to the same university, keep together. Nothing was going to tear us apart. One day, maybe marriage and children. The whole expected dream.

I got scared by that.

Ran. Ending what we had after three years with a text message. That's how you run like a professional shitebag.

I ran from university too. Claiming it was for a higher purpose. That I realised I wanted to be a cop. Uni was not for me. I could better serve my life by joining up. All shite, of course. I just got scared I wasn't smart enough. Or that I'd screw up at the last second.

I spent my career in the force skipping through assignments, transferring every chance I got, looking for something and then getting scared I might find it.

The question was, what was I running from?

I don't know. Whenever I get comfortable, whenever things seemed to be going well, this little voice in my head says *run*. Sit me down with a psychoanalyst, we might sort it out. But then I'd run before the therapy finished. Because I wouldn't know what else to do.

Burke and Crawford approached me. They knew my files, but saw something they thought they could use. They backed me into a corner, surrounded me, made me seriously consider what their operation had to offer. They thought they had me on the ropes. Thought they had me in the one place I couldn't run.

And, for a while, I agreed with them.

Going undercover meant re-creating myself, abandoning everything I had and inhabiting a new life. It felt good. Felt right. I was a natural because I'd been doing that all of my life.

If I kept running I didn't have to think about letting anyone down or about dealing with the consequences of my actions. I was gone before anything mattered.

And then I met Kat. I was supposed to fake falling for her. But what happened was something between us clicked, and all of a

199

sudden, I didn't want to run. But in staying still, I messed things up even more. Drove her away.

It had been temporary, like all things. I should have seen it, should have known it couldn't be any other way. And now, here I am, running again when all I wanted to do was stay where I was.

• • •

I'm on John Knox heading for Duke Street when the jam sandwich brigade squeal past. They don't even think twice about the ordinary little motor I'm driving. Chances are I'm just some drone hoping to get home and get a few hours' sleep before getting up early and heading back to work. The hopeless, everyday grind that the police are supposed to protect and serve.

Keep us in our place.

Keep the ordinary Joes in line.

I shake my head. Jesus, thinking like one of those mental cases you get yelling on Sauchie from on top their wee boxes about the exploitation of the working classes and the conspiracy of Government.

I have to keep my head straight. Focus on my goal. And I try. God knows I try. But inside my head, it's like I'm split in two. Dual identities finally coming apart. Fighting for dominance.

The undercover cop. The would-be criminal. The killer.

I can't look in the rear view, not knowing who'll look back at me.

But the answer's painfully obvious.

I get back to Partick, park poorly. Tense feeling in my stomach. Like it's collapsing in on itself. My brain insists I'm being watched.

They're here for you.

They're inside the flat.

I don't know if 'they' are the cops or the criminals. The main players are dead, doesn't mean someone isn't out for revenge.

But there's no-one there. No-one waiting for me. No handcuffs. No guns.

Inside the front door, I pause, take out my phone and swap SIM cards for the last time. Send a message. One final declaration. Maybe an apology of sorts. I think of it like a case summary, a way of explaining what happened.

I have to do something. They have to know I didn't become one of the bad guys. That I was still thinking like police, no matter how bad my decisions wound up being.

I think again. Put in my personal SIM. Is Kat's number still the same? Is she even still alive? I send the message anyway. What does it matter?

Then I take the phone and drop it down the toilet. It's useless now. A burden.

I head for the bedroom, the walk-in. False back I found when I moved in. I remove the panel, look at the bricks wrapped in plastic. Money I took in hand from Tony for certain services and never bothered declaring to Crawford. All lumped up, finally ready to be used.

I think about the message I sent to Kat.

Hope she'll accept this feeble replacement for an apology.

Because I know, after tonight, for her, even Oban won't be far enough.

Kat

There are needles in my arm. People are talking. I hear voices. But they don't make any sense. I'm lying on a hard surface. There's a blanket covering me.

Am I in bed? Why are there other people in the room?

Someone leans over me. A man. His voice is low. I think it's meant to be soothing. I struggle to hear him. Blink to bring his face into focus.

'Kat? Do you know who I am?

He looks familiar. But he's half hidden in the shadows, and his voice is too distorted for me to recognise.

The world is shaking. There's a high-pitched noise in my head. No, not my head. Somewhere else. Outside.

I blink. Think: this is an ambulance.

Realise: I'm alive.

I try to focus on the man's features. They're familiar. Definitely. I've seen them before. A long time ago.

Where?

My flat. My old place. The one that Uncle Derek owned.

Yes, this man was in my front room. I wanted to throw him out, but I was too polite, and maybe even too afraid of what he had to say to me.

The policeman. The detective.

Crawford.

'Do you remember me?'

Aye, of course I do.

Do I say that out loud?

He's softer than I remember. In attitude if not shape. There's a little middle-age spread that I don't remember, and the lines in his face seem more pronounced. But all that could be my imagination. We knew each other for little more than fifteen minutes back then. And I didn't want to remember him at all when he left.

He says, 'Where's John?'

'Why don't you ask him?' Comes out like I'm trying to slap him, we're in a bar and I'm throwing my drink in his face.

I always wanted to throw my drink in someone's face. Never did. Little regrets like that. Maybe everyone has them.

'I know he was there tonight. We didn't see his body.'

I laugh, taste something thick and warm in the back of my throat and swallow it back.

He nods, trying to hide it, look sage, like Alec Guinness in the *Star Wars* films, but he's rattled.

'I see. You didn't see anything?'

'Was he one of yours?'

'One of mine?'

'Did you send him to infiltrate my uncle's operations?'

He doesn't say anything.

'Did you instruct him to use me to get close to my uncle?'

Again, nothing. But there's a twitch. I can see it. His right eye. And he won't look directly at me, either.

'Isn't that,' I say, 'against the rules?'

'The rules?'

'He was undercover. I thought there were rules. You know, things that you can and can't do.'

'We keep rewriting the rules. I don't think there are any. Not really.' He looks a little sad, as though he wishes there really were clear lines to separate the good guys from the bad in such a situation.

I cough. It hurts. My upper body spasms. I think I feel something inside me tear. Someone else leans over me now. Dressed in the green of a paramedic. 'If you're going to upset her...'

'Not my intention.'

We hit a corner. The weight shifts in the ambulance. It's like hitting the apex on a rollercoaster. Except more scary than fun.

The man in green pulls away. Crawford leans in.

'No-one wanted to mislead you. John needed to get close because your cousins, your uncle, all those bastards. They trust you, and we needed them to trust him. You're the one good person in their lives. It was a good tactic. Far as these things go. I signed off on it. But it was never supposed to go this far.'

'What did you think he was going to do? Hang around forever?'

'The operation was originally budgeted for six months.'

I try not to laugh. It will only hurt.

'Your uncle was a tough man to reach. Keeps himself insulated. Guess you know that, though.'

'Maybe he didn't do all those things that you –' He doesn't have to interrupt me. I stop myself, realising how I sound. I can't do it any more. Can't keep lying to myself, never mind anyone else.

'Where is John?' He looks me in the eye now. Insistent. Like I'm not telling him something.

'He hasn't reported in? Come back to his masters?'

'No. Where is he?'

What's the point in lying? 'He's gone. Took off before you arrived.'

'Took off?'

What is he? A parrot or a detective?

But Crawford's starting to assemble the jigsaw. A lightbulb flutters behind those grey eyes.

'Kat.' Making sure he has my full attention. 'Who killed your cousins?'

Let him work for it. Old habits die hard. Can hear the old me: *the police are the enemy. Don't give them anything.* But he's working it out for himself. I can hear the gears turning. I'm telling him but I haven't told him anything.

'Who killed them?'

He doesn't give up.

He's not even waiting for an answer. Leaning forward, in my face. 'Kat, you have to trust me. If I knew... He's been on the edge for months, we knew that. It was getting to him. The double life. The lies. Maybe because of how he felt about you. And how you left him the way you did. We thought maybe he was taking drugs to stay on your cousin's good side... Would explain a lot about how he started behaving... But I wonder maybe it was the fact he to lied to you, and that you saw through it.'

John always told me he was clean, that he wouldn't use. Didn't mind if other people did, but you know, he had his own personal standards. I wonder when he started. Before or after I left? Of course, just being near Tony could give you contact high.

'He's been slipping, losing his grip. Finding it tough to remember the line between cop and cover.'

Did I know anything about John? Or was everything I thought

I knew a lie, part of the persona he created?

I used to think I knew his soul. Now I have to wonder.

'Kat, he went over the edge. Tonight he plummeted somewhere very dark indeed. Maybe a culmination of everything he's been through. Maybe because he was trying to save you. Keeping quiet isn't protecting him or anyone else. I can only imagine what you've been through this evening. I know that...'

'Did they find her?' I ask.

'What?'

'Lesley.'

He looks at me with his head cocked to one side. The name means nothing to him.

'Lesley Scott.' I rattle off her address. 'Did they find her?'

'I don't...'

'I watched her die. He... Ray...put a bullet in her head. She was trying to call the police. Only doing what she thought was the right thing.' There's a tightness in my chest. I start to breathe faster.

That's it. I'm gone. Going.

Heart's overheating. The world is shaking. That keening noise is too high, threatens to burst my eardrums. I shake and shiver and there are tears, and I know if I even try to talk I won't make any sense at all.

A beep-beep-beep noise cracks from somewhere, and the man in green pulls Crawford away from me. Good. I want him gone. Just need to be left alone.

The world starts to crack around the edges.

'Jesus! Hurry it up! Hurry the fuck up!'

The world starts to go dark. Do ambulances have dimmer switches?

'Hold on, Kat. Hold on. Don't let it end like this.' Someone's holding my hand. I look up at them. Crawford's face is creased with what looks like genuine concern. His grey eyes are watery.

The world blacks out.

I bring it back into focus.
Crawford is gone.
I see my mother. She smiles.
And I'm gone.

Where Will You Run

Two days after the funeral

0930 – 1000

John

The minutes are shorter. The seconds click by faster than I can notice.

Drugs?

Tony had a point. They take the edge off. When it counts. I'd been dancing. Teetering. Ready to fall. Drink wasn't enough.

Nothing was enough.

Maybe the psycho had a point, after all. I'm glad he left his stash in the car. A snort, and I could almost believe he was beside me, egging me on, telling me he couldn't trust a man who didn't take a little hit every now and then.

But he's not beside me. He's dead. I blew his fucking brains out.

So I'm buzzing as the taxi pulls up outside the main concourse. On the right side, faceless, charmless airport hotels as exciting as plastic shells overlook the terminal building. Frankenstein's monsters of construction, they loom, not quite alive.

I pay the taxi, tell him he can keep the change, which is well over five quid above the odds. He objects, but I figure it's fair enough, given the way the day has been going.

Maybe when he watches the telly later, he'll have a wee story tell folks. 'You'll never guess who I had in the back of my cab...'

All the calm from earlier has vanished. In its place there's an effervescent sense of danger. Excitement. Where am I heading?

I need to keep the plan straight in my head. The drugs take the edge off, but they don't half screw with joined up thinking.

Cyprus. Easy to hide. Tony had some contacts there. I know their names. Figure dropping his name will help. No-one's going to know what I did. At least not for a while. Even when Crawford connects the dots, he's going to want to keep things quiet. I'm his operation's dirty wee stain. He'll want to ignore me as long as he can, pretend I never even existed.

I need to get my head together, get time to think.

Best to do that in the sun, right?

The girl at the desk looks at me with an odd expression when I ask for a ticket on the next flight out to Paphos. The look screams suspicion. Most tickets are booked on the internet these days, but then if they didn't want business done like this, they'd have closed the desks. I've got enough left in my old account to cover the flights. Can sort the rest out once I get to Cyprus. Enough money in my checked luggage to keep me safe for a while. I can exchange some on the other side of the gates. Long as customs play dumb.

Getting through security, my stomach shrinks and threatens to double me right over. Reminds me of when I was a boy, my appendix blowing up. That same early stinging sensation that grew more and painful, became this overwhelming agony flooring me more effectively than a right hook from Muhammed Ali in his prime.

Right now it was simple discomfort. A stress reaction.

Keep thinking: *once you're in the air, you're fine.*

The lines are long. Security since 9/11 has become a pain in the arse, all these airlines terrified about terrorism. Truth is, someone determined enough, could probably get away with anything, no matter how many security measures were put in place. Most security is more about insurance than genuine protection of innocent lives.

'Take off your belt.'

I don't even notice I'm next to the scanners. I stare blankly at the guy in the security uniform. He stares back, intense. That military style buzz doesn't help with the intimidation. 'Please, take off your belt. Your shoes are fine.'

Of course they are, I'm wearing canvas trainers. My old clothes – the bloodstained ones – I left at the flat. What was the point in covering my tracks? All I have to hope is the fake passport I'm using is enough for me to breeze through the rest of the way.

I take off my belt, put it in the tray. Move forward.

So close.

Through the machines. Out the other side. All I have to do.

I grab a coffee at a café, which has bay windows looking out onto the tarmac. I watch the planes as they taxi to the runways.

What they represent: freedom. Absolute freedom.

Nothing more freeing than breaking from gravity. Even if it is inside a confined metal tube. There's something about knowing the ground is so far beneath you that is both terrifying and wonderful.

I have three hours to kill.

Three fucking hours.

To shite with the coffee. Where's the bar?

•   •   •

Ray looks at me with empty eyes.

Literally empty. Nothing in those sockets except blank space.

He clambers to his feet. His joints crack. Blood soaks his clothes. His limbs move unnaturally, and I think of a spider with its long, multi-jointed limbs.

He tries to speak, but for some reason can't make a sound. Maybe something to do with all those worms in his mouth, wriggling, writhing, struggling to break free.

Beside him, Tony is touching the hole in the back of his head, fingers probing gently as though afraid he'll damage himself.

'You're a shitebag,' Tony says. His voice is muffled, like he's speaking through a mouthful of dirt.

I don't see anything. I just sit on the bench and look at the two of them.

Brothers. Killers.

'Don't judge me,' I say. 'I did what I had to do.'

'Did what you wanted,' Tony says. 'Big fuckin' difference, pal.'

Ray says, 'It's a sickness. The violence.' His voice slams like heavy church doors. Worms fall from his lips. Same hollow feeling of quiet when he stops speaking.

I stand up. When I look round, the bench is gone.

Tony comes up to me. 'You didn't do anything you didn't want to.'

'It's a sickness,' Ray says again.

'Shut up, you fuck,' Tony says. 'You piece of shit. You're not my brother. You're a monster.'

Another voice: 'My monster.'

Their father stands between them. There's a hole in the middle of his forehead. Blood trickles across his porcelain white skin. Ray doesn't respond. He never does. Not really. Only time I saw him angry was in the hospital, when he felt someone had betrayed him.

But he's right. It's a sickness, the violence. Transmittable. It gets inside you, makes you the kind of person you never wanted to be.

'No-one made you do anything,' Tony says.

I want to argue with him, but then something inside me lurches sickeningly and I wonder if maybe he's right.

Ray says, 'It's a sickness. You're born with it.'

My stomach cramps. Like when I was a kid. I double over. Vomit blood. It splashes on the grass at my feet.

The grass is brown. Too much sun, not enough rain.

Tony says, 'Better than fertiliser.'

I'm on my knees. My stomach is agony. I press it in as though that will help the pain. Something pushes back.

'You're born with it,' Ray says with that slamming, heavy voice that isn't his.

The something inside me erupts. Pulls its way out. Ripping through flesh. I hear a noise like paper being torn in two. I fall back onto the ground. Don't look. Don't want to see what this cancerous thing is that's killing me.

When I open my eyes, I'm blinded by the sun that shines in the impossibly blue and clear sky.

The old man is standing over me.

'You're the son I never had,' he says.

I try to scream.

211

• • •

I'm falling.

My eyes snap open. Hands grasp out for something to hold onto.

But I'm not falling. I'm just asleep in the bar, my pint half-finished in front of me.

I think I'm going to be sick, but I manage to steady myself. Standing up, I'm dizzy and think I might not even be able to walk.

But I do it. Each step increases my confidence. Leaves the nightmare behind.

Check out the departures board. Gate 3.

I make the trip. Walking slowly. Just a nightmare. I'll have more than a few of those over the next wee while, I'm sure.

At the gate, I get my passport ready. They're calling for boarding.

I'm so close. Can see the plane out the window.

My freedom.

This is it.

A hand clamps my shoulder. I twist. Breathe in.

Crawford grins. 'You're coming in, son,' he says. 'It's over.'

The uniforms behind him raise their weapons enough that I notice. Armed police. Making the point absolutely clear.

Crawford keeps his hands on my shoulder. 'I'm here to help you, son.'

I swallow.

'She's alive. You know that, right? She's alive, son. Kat Scobie.'

I smile. Then I pull my shoulder away from his grasp, and bring my knee up. Catch him in the groin, and he folds. I pull away.

The officers raise their weapons. Like they're going to fire in here.

People scatter. No-one knows what they're doing.

Perfect.

Am I still dreaming?

I push past the girl in the cabin crew outfit, stumble down the umbilical corridor that leads to the plane. I'm not boarding, but I need out and this is my nearest available bastarding exit.

At the far end, there's a gap and a drop.

Too far?

I slip between the end of the umbilical and the plane.

Someone's shouting.

I perform a hanging drop. Same way you're taught to leave a burning building. Tuck and land, absorb the impact with bent knees. My body trembles with shock. My feet roar with pain. I fall onto my side. The tarmac is surprisingly cool.

Someone's shouting from above. I can't make out the words. Don't give a fuck.

I get up, start running. Under the nose of the plane, across the tarmac. My ankles protest. Less a sprint and more a lurch.

'Where are you going, John? Where are you going, John?'

It becomes a mantra, a way of breathing, controlling speed, finding focus. Muttered between the ice cold stabs of air that attack my lungs.

'Where are you going, John?'

I just know that I need to keep running. I make the mistake of turning, see the airport police running from the terminal.

HK automatic rifles. Body armour. That's modern air travel for you.

They're running with the enthusiasm of the under-used. Have they seen action? Jesus, do they know I'm unarmed? Do they give a toss? I pick up the pace.

I'm cocooned by the roar of jet engines from planes on runways all around. I run. Blind. If I don't know where I'm going, neither do they. Every time my feet slap the tarmac, the ice stabs my lungs.

It would be so easy to give in. But I have to run.

The scream of engines gets louder. I bow my head and keep going. Is this how I want to go? Butch Cassidy, just without the Sundance Kid?

'Where are you going, John?' The words burst out jagged and

uneven, starting to hurt with each repetition.

The air around me trembles. A dark shadow comes from nowhere.

I look up, see the tail of a turning plane just in front of me. Heading away.

I keep running.

Don't look back.

Keep –

It's a solid wall of air, like running into concrete. I slam to a halt, then bounce back. Lifted off my feet. At first there's no pain, but I'm aware of something in my chest cracking. I look down and see that I'm off the ground. I'm floating. Flying. Free.

The ground looms. I close my eyes. The roaring intensifies. My eardrums burst. All I hear is the roar. It becomes my world. Blanks out every other experience.

And there's no pain.

No pain. For a moment, that surprises me.

And then:

There's nothing.

Three weeks later

Kat

I watch his belongings burn. The stuff that they left behind.

The police took John's possessions.

Evidence.

Without his testimony – how can a man talk after he's been caught in the stream of a jet engine? – they need to piece together what happened.

What's left – paltry, meagre, next to nothing – I'm burning.

I don't know if it makes me feel better.

I don't know what I'm going to do. I have savings, but not much. And Crawford and the solicitors keep telling me I can't go too far. Back to Oban, maybe. The life I made there. But I know it was never really home, just a place where I could try and gather myself. Now, I think maybe there's nothing for me there.

I'm a material witness. They need me to stick around.

I didn't tell them about the text message he sent me the night of Ray's funeral.

If he had something for me, then I wanted to see it first. Thinking maybe it would help me understand him, whether he really was the man that I thought I loved.

I still have a key to John's place. Sentimental? Or just that I didn't know what to do with it?

I take a look around the bedroom. It's bare now. The bed is just a frame with an old mattress. After I left, it seems that he went back to basics. Living like a monk in a cell. Only the essentials. Nothing more than that.

I look at the walk in cupboard. The doors are open. There's something wrong at the back wall. Like he said in the message. I step in, tug at the loose board.

Bending down hurts. Every movement is stiff and painful, still. But I figure I need to do this on my own. It can only hurt for so long.

The cupboard extends further back than I realised. There's a whole other storage space in there. Empty except for a battered old sports bag.

I pull it out. Throw it on the mattress. Watch it bounce. The effort's nearly too much. I'm short of breath. I sit down and take a moment. Then I undo the zipper. Figure the painkillers are too strong; I'm hallucinating.

The notes aren't fake. I'm a Scobie. I've seen fake. I've seen marked.

I smile, thinking about when I was sixteen, took some money

my uncle had lying around on his kitchen worktop. I was arrested in Woolworths. Jesus, the humiliation. Made worse by my uncle coming down the station to 'sort everything out' and by getting away as though the incident had never happened. Even worse, getting a grudging apology from the officer who had responded to the incident and slapped the cuffs on me.

I look at the money in the bag. Shake my head.

Does it really make up for everything? Did he think it would matter to me?

How much? Two hundred thousand? Conservative guess.

I think about John buying that ticket. Looking to start a new life. Is this his way of apologising?

There's a note in the bag too. I know his handwriting. I rip the paper into tiny pieces without bothering to read his scrawl.

Finally, I allow myself a smile. Sit next to the bag on the bed.

Plan my own escape. This time, making it real. Oban was almost a pretence, a way of escaping without really leaving. This time, I have the chance to start over again. No family left. No ties, no lingering sentimentality.

I can leave. Be whoever I want.

Scabies Scobie?

Kat Scobie?

Does it matter? It's a big world out there. Two hundred thousand isn't much in the grand scheme of the world.

But it's a start.

Acknowledgements

Ray's inability to feel pain is based in part on a real condition (known as HSAN, or sometimes Congenital Insensitivity to Pain). I have however taken a number of liberties with the condition in the name of dramatic licence. As ever, any errors are my own.

With thanks to:

Sara Hunt at Saraband for taking a chance on this new book and being so enthusiastic. I've been a fan of the Contraband line for a while, so delighted to now be part of the gang.

Al Guthrie, as ever, for his support and assistance through the writing of this book, and for helping it to find a home.

Louise Hutcheson for some of the kindest editorial notes I've ever had.

Jay Stringer and James Oswald, who read early drafts of this work and didn't tell me to give up right there and then.

All my friends, associates and fellow miscreants who provide the kind of invisible support without which I wouldn't be able to keep working. Special shout-out to the Long Promised Cameo – you know who you are!

Booksellers and librarians everywhere.

You, the reader, especially if you actually got this far and bothered to read all the nattering nonsense in the acknowledgements. That is dedication above and beyond the call of duty.

Mum and Dad – still no French house, but maybe a bottle of French wine…

Mycroft, Magwitch and Moriarty – because of course I'm mad enough to thank the cats.

And, of course, Lesley McDowell – let's crack open some prosecco!